The Power Affair

In memory of
Robert S. Miller
6-19-1946 to 8-10-1983

By Zeke Crandall

Soft bound signed copies of The Power Affair are available for sale through Amazon, Kindle and createspace.com.

All of my books can also be purchased from the author direct and are all addressed and signed by the author. Our website is www.arizonatales.com or by simply emailing the author with purchases. Our email address is www.arizonatales.com.

Other books that are currently available through the author if not seen on Amazon, Kindle or Create space are; Arizona Tales, Arizona Train Robbers, The Simple Man, Ghost in the Desert, Canyon Diablo and Pleasant Valley Revisited.

Thank You
Zeke Crandall

Preface

It was July in the year 1966. I had just purchased a new 1965 Ford Mustang convertible from Sanderson Ford, in Glendale, Arizona. I worked at Cummins Diesel while going to high school and planned to continue my employment until I completed my college education. My manager, Keith Parks at Cummins Diesel, referred me to Don Stallard, the fleet salesman for Sanderson. Keith said I would get a better deal if I worked with John, due to the huge volume of vehicles Cummins bought from him. The Mustang was considered new because it was driven by a dealership executive. It only had 7,000 miles on it when I took possession.

The author pledged the Tau Omega Fraternity my second year at Phoenix College and I became good friends with two of the members, Craig Gunderson and George Sevy. The three of us decided to take a road trip to Prescott for the Fourth of July Rodeo weekend festivities. I picked Craig and George up at our fraternity house on 1st Street, just south of McDowell Road, a little after three on a Friday afternoon. Our Prescott party destination was Whiskey Row in downtown Prescott. We stopped at a Circle K, filled my gas tank and bought a case of Miller beer, in cans, for the trip. We took the back road going north through the rural towns of Wickenburg then Yarnell, Peoples Valley, Kirkland Junction and up through the mountains for about thirty-five miles to Prescott. Interstate 17, was about the same distance and a little faster. However, we thought the winding roads would give us a chance to see how well my new sports car would do on its initial test run. On rural roads the speed limit is 25 mph, but I don't think I went much under 50 for the whole trip.

Unexpectedly, at the junction of Interstate 89 and the Skull Valley Road, we had a blowout of the right rear tire. We hobbled into a service station that was only about a hundred yards north of the intersection. It was about four thirty in the afternoon, and sure enough, the darn service station was closed. After we came to a complete stop the three of us piled out of the car to assess the damage and prepared to change the tire ourselves. We each only had one change of clothes and we didn't want to get dirty changing the tire.

I am sure we were a sight for sore eyes, standing there looking like we had our thumbs up our butts trying to figure out how we were going to change that darn tire. Lucky for us, a homemade buckboard, constructed with car axles and regular rubber tires, being pulled by two horses and carrying three real old cowboys pulled up next to us. As we turned our heads to see the wagon one of the men sitting on the bench seat with the reins in his hand asked, "Hey guys you look like you can use a little help." They could see we were in trouble and not exactly dressed for the emergency. We were dressed to the hilt in our 1960's hippy, party attire. We wore bell bottom pants, crepe shirts and all of us were wearing Beatle Boots, the semi-platform, ankle high boots that zipped up the side. We all had long hair and mustaches. We certainly looked out of place in those rural Arizona surroundings. One of the old guys introduced himself as Tom. He was the one who asked us if we needed help; Tom introduced us to his older brother John and their mutual friend Lee, who was a long time friend and the foreman of a nearby cattle ranch where they all were employed.

The men offered to help change the tire and when we agreed, the three of them jumped off the buckboard. The bigger man, Tom, was the first to speak, saying;

"Get out of our way boys and we will have this tire changed in no time!"

The job would have taken us an hour but they were through changing the tire in fewer than ten minutes. To show them our appreciation, we invited them into a nearby bar to buy them each a cold beer as a gesture of our gratitude. As we drank our beer Tom told us about their jobs working on at cattle ranch a few miles away and their friend Lee, who was the head wrangler of the spread.

Tom went on to explain that he and his brother John had been released from the Florence State Prison, where they had spent some forty-two years, incarcerated for crimes that they said they did not commit. He emphasized, they were thrilled to be out of prison, glad to have jobs and were simply enjoying their freedom.

I was going to inquire about their crimes and why they had such a long prison sentence, but figured maybe I had better leave it alone. I asked them if they knew Jerry Paxton, who was one of my neighborhood buddies that was incarcerated at the same prison. They told us they knew him; I got real concerned because Jerry had told me stories about the homosexual lifestyle that went on in that prison. I felt very uncomfortable as they smiled at us. They seemed like nice guys but the way we were dressed, they probably thought we were queer. George and I went to the restroom and I told him about my friend Jerry and the sick crap that went on in prison. We were convinced they wanted to have sex with us, so we decided to get the heck out of there after we finished our beers. We told the brothers we needed to be on our way before it got dark. We thanked them for helping us. We bought them another round of beers, said goodbye and left, getting out of there as fast as our bell-bottomed legs could carry us.

We finally arrived in Prescott around seven o'clock that Friday evening. We checked into our room at the

St Michaels Hotel. Our room was on the second floor which overlooked Montezuma Street, known as Whiskey Row. The name came about when the town founders established an ordinance that only allowed bars, gambling businesses, and brothels to be located on Montezuma Street, just between Gurley and Goodwin Streets. The city wanted the revenue, but they wanted to limit all of the gambling, drinking, and the sporting ladies to a specific designated area, to control such elements and protect their families from such elements.

The main draw in Prescott during the 4th of July was the rodeo, the rodeo dance, and the holiday parade. People were allowed to throw water balloons on the people in the parade, and we had the perfect room. We could fill up our water balloons in our room sink and toss the balloons on the folks in the parade outside the front window that overlooked Whiskey Row. Sadly, that practice has since been long forgotten by the Prescott City Council; probably because, in later years, people were throwing balloons filled with urine. However, for us, it was pure fun just to throw water balloons on the people getting everybody wet and cooled in the July heat.

We brought the rest of the unopened beer up to our room. They were in cans with the pull off tabs; such progress from the old church key cans. We ate a late dinner downstairs in the hotel the dinning room. After dinner we went back up to our room and finished the rest of the beer so we would be ready for the rodeo dance that was to take place right below on Montezuma Street. Both ends of Whiskey Row were blocked off and a mobile stage was moved in place just south of Gurley Street. There were lots of tables and chairs in the street along with six different locations where alcoholic drinks were being served. The dance went from nine o'clock to Midnight after which we hit the bars on Whiskey Row and drank until closing time at 1 o'clock. What a great, no, groovy time we had.

Jumping ahead, in 1985, I was researching information for one of my books when I came across a short story in an Arizona Highways magazine, from 1964. It told about a famous gun battle that took place in 1918 at Rattlesnake Canyon within the Galiuro Mountains near the town of Klondyke, Arizona. Gold diggers coming back from the Alaskan gold fields founded and named the town thinking it would be good luck to call it Klondike, but they misspelled the name, as it remains today. The surrounding area of Aravaipa Valley, was bordered on the north by Mount Graham, west by the Galiuro and Aravaipa mountain ranges then to the east by the Pinaleno mountain range. The valley ran about 40 miles across and 80 miles from the north to the south.

Studying several old pictures in the article, I recognized the two brothers we had met on the way to Prescott in 1966. Sure enough, they were the same two men who changed our tire and drank with us. They were quite a bit older when we met them but they definitely were the same two men. I went on to find that Tom and John Power, along with their father Jeff Power and a hired hand, "Big Tom Sisson" had all participated in the shootout at Rattlesnake Canyon some 12 miles east of Klondyke and about 30 miles north of Fort Grant in the Aravaipai Valley within Graham County.

The shootout occurred during the early morning on February 10th 1918. I was amused to affirm, reading the article, neither of the men was queer and realized my friends and I had had nothing to fear from them. I continued my research looking for newspaper and magazine articles to help me understand the circumstances surrounding this amazing gunfight, one I never knew existed until I found that Arizona Highways article. It was too bad I hadn't taken the time to listen more closely to those old timers; I am sure they could have filled my ears for hours with the true story of what actually happened to them that fateful cold morning almost eighty years ago. I especially regret it now because I am sure they would have been able to provide valuable information that has been inaccurately recorded or undiscovered over the years.

During the past fifteen years I have read every newspaper article from each paper published in the state of Arizona along with old Arizona Highways' articles, additional magazine articles and every book with any information about the deadliest gunfight, and largest manhunt in Arizona history. No less amazing is the fact that Tom and John Power served the longest prison sentences recorded in Arizona. The same 42 years they told me in 1966. The transcripts of the trial have mysteriously disappeared along with an inquest performed on the body of Ola May Power, Tom and John's baby sister, whose death still remains a mystery.

I wish to thank my good friend Tom McCarthy, a homicide detective in Chicago for twenty years. Tom handled an average case load of 200 murders a year and was responsible for the investigation and arrest in each case, resulting in one of the highest conviction records in Chicago history. Tom's amazing investigative background together with my research, allowed us to put the pieces together as best as possible since most of the evidence has been destroyed or has been conveniently misplaced.

I personally hiked into the sites of the Garden and Power cabins in February of 1996, during the same time periods of the gunfight. I spent the night on February 9th in the Garden cabin so I could be awake at dawn the next morning; I wanted to see what the lighting would have been at dawn that morning in 1918.

All of the records concerning the death of Ola May Power in December 1917, just two months before the actual gunfight took place, have disappeared. Tom McCarthy and I believe that her mysterious death along with several other issues had a lot to do with the unfortunate gunfight. However, this incident put a unique stain on Arizona's early history.

Written records and witness testimony state the shooting started just after daybreak, around seven a.m. There would have been enough light on that fateful morning, when all parties would have been able to see and clearly distinguish each other. This unnecessary gunfight never should have occurred, but did thanks to hot tempers, fright, greed and one combatant who brought an untested weapon with a hair trigger.

Most of what you will read is true, but since all of the parties involved in the gunfight have long passed and all of the records have disappeared, I could only rely on newspaper articles, the inquest records, prison records and the out-of-print book that was written by Tom Power.

To the best of my knowledge after fifteen years of research, I present this amazing story of the last most unnecessary gunfight, largest manhunt, and the longest prison sentences recorded in Arizona history.

I am so grateful to Tom Power for keeping his personal journal which made this intriguing story possible. In addition, I'm thankful for all the historical documents that were so carefully preserved all these years which verified this amazing part of Arizona history.

This book includes many photos and copied newspaper articles allowing the reader insight into the old-west Arizona before and after this tragic historical event.

All photos in this book are compliments of *www.arizonahiking.org* with their permission to use in this book. The balance of the photos used in this book were taken by this author.

Arizona joined the Union of American States on February 14th, 1912. When this shootout took place, February 10th, 1918, we had been a state just under six years. Arizona was a vast uninhabited land area. The only real population was then, as it is today, in the larger towns of Phoenix, Tucson, Prescott and Flagstaff. The total population of the State of Arizona in 1918 was 335,000. Safford, the capital of Graham County, was one of many small towns. It was founded in the 1870's along with several other towns in the eastern part of the state including Show Low, Pinetop, Taylor, Greer. Most of the small towns in Graham and Greenlee counties were founded by Mormon settlers. Horses and wagons were still the main means of transportation. It's hard to imagine but the automobile was a rare and costly luxury at that time.

The author would like to thank Joe Schuler for creating this cover from a picture the author took while visiting the site of the gun battle and my friend Bobby Carsten for editing this book.

Chapter One

The year was 1890. The Power family lived on a 320 acre cattle ranch in West Texas about one hundred miles, northeast of Austin, near the New Mexico border. Twenty acres of their ranch was used for growing crops and the rest of the ranch was needed to support 1,150 cattle and 30 horses. Jeff Power was considered wealthy by all standards at that time. One had to be tough and self-reliant to survive because the land was primitive and harsh. It was a land of extremes, where stock, farms, and lives were often wiped out by such natural events as drought, followed often by heavy rains, and often pestilence. The human disasters came about from greed, desire for power, and violence.

Thomas Jefferson Power, who liked to be called by his middle name "Jeff," was a man of his time. He was born and raised in West Texas. He knew horses, cattle, guns and the daily struggle to provide a living for himself, his wife Martha Morgan, their infant son Charles and his widowed mother, Martha Jane who lived with the family after Jeff's father had passed away in the flu epidemic of 1887. Hereafter, since both Jeff's wife and mother were named Martha, his wife Martha Morgan will be distinguished from Grandma Jane to avoid confusion. History and other writers have confused certain facts about these women because of the identical first names.

Following the flu epidemic West Texas suffered a three-year drought. Finally, after the third year, having lost most of their crops and nearly all of their cattle, Jeff decided it was time to move farther west to find land that would allow them to grow plenty of crops and raise more cattle. In the spring of 1891 Jeff rounded up the surviving one hundred-fifty head of cattle and remaining horses. He loaded two wagons with his family, their belongings, and together with a young neighbor, Johnny Sherd, they left Texas and headed into the New Mexico Territory.

The Power family arrived in the settlement of Cliff, in Grant County, New Mexico sometime in late May of 1891. Jeff had enough money saved to purchase a 160-acre ranch of which he immediately transformed 17 acres into a farming area so the family could cultivate the land to grow and sell their own vegetable crops. Soon after, he went to work for LC Land & Cattle Company, while the ranch and crops matured. His wife and mother maintained the crops, the cattle, chickens, and hogs.

Later that year the Duck Creek Range War, that had been going off and on for several years between rival cattlemen and sheep herders broke out again after five years of peace. Following several shootings, Jeff feared for his life and those of his loved ones. So, he quit the job and expanded his own ranch trying to build it up so the family could survive without him having to take jobs that would keep him away from his family.

On November 11, 1891 Martha Morgan Power gave birth to a second son, John Grant Power. On May 16th 1893 came a third son, Thomas Jefferson Jr., called Tom. On November 29th 1894, Martha gave birth to the last of the Power children, and only daughter, Ola May.

The family prospered for the next six years; their cattle had tripled to a herd of over 450 along with six bulls. Jeff purchased another 320 acres of adjacent land from a nearby rancher whose herd had simply outgrown his own ranch. Jeff decided to lease a portion of his newly acquired additional land, to a farmer named James Reede. As part of the lease agreement James was to share the crops when harvest time came. Jeff was then able to concentrate his time on building up his cattle herd.

Reede immediately began building his own ranch house about 400 yards away from Power home. He first erected two large-forked posts to hold a ridge-pole, followed by heavy logs for rafters, covering them with brush, grass, and finally a thick layer of dirt to finish the roof. The day he completed the house, Martha and grandma Jane went to inspect the new dwelling and with them they brought a few house warming gifts to "dress it up a bit." Shortly after they went into the home, the ridge-pole collapsed, burying them. Grandma Jane was unhurt and was able to quickly dig herself out from under the wreckage. However, Martha had been struck in the head by the falling ridge pole and was pinned beneath the all the rubble of the fallen roof.

James Reede, who had been standing in the doorway, was also unhurt. Grandma Jane began screaming at him to help her dig Martha out of the debris. Apparently Reede was so shocked he remained unmoving in the doorway, petrified. Grandma Power ran toward her house shouting for her son, but Jeff, who had heard the screams and thundering sounds of the crashing roof, had burst out of his house and was running toward his mother. She hollered;

"The roof fell in, Jeff, and Martha's under it!"

Reede was still standing in the doorway when Jeff and Grandma Jane got there. Jeff literally had to push James aside in order to get into the house. Reede must have snapped out of his daze, because he was right there next to Jeff helping him lift the ridge pole, and dig through the dirt to uncover Martha. Sadly. she was dead and it was thought by all that she must have died instantly from massive head injuries when the ridge pole had struck her. Crying, Jeff held his dead wife in his arms rocking her back and forth.

The following day Jeff's beloved wife, Martha Morgan, was buried in the back yard of the Power home. She had often commented to Grandma Jane that she would never want to be buried in the town cemetery because badgers were always caught digging up the graves. She said she knew she would be safe if she was buried at home.

Following Martha's death, Jeff suffered a major depression and nothing in his life seemed to have meaning according to his son, Charles. Jeff was only twenty- eight years old but still tough and stubborn. He became very restless looking at his wife's grave every day and soon sold the ranch including his entire herd of cattle. He gathered up his mother and his four children and began one of those seemingly aimless odysseys, which were very typical of pioneers in the early American west.

The family first moved back to Texas, then on to Oklahoma and finally moved to Kansas. On a desolate Kansas prairie, they came across a deserted sod home. After inspecting the ranch, Jeff's first statement, when they moved into their new home was;

> "It's forty miles to wood; sixty miles to water, God bless our home!"

After an unsuccessful year living in Kansas, the family picked up roots once again; they kept moving, first to Colorado, back to New Mexico and again to Texas. Jeff worked at whatever jobs he could find; being frugal, having saved the money he got from selling his ranch, he kept an eye open for a ranch that had promise, but he never found a spread he liked. While in El Paso, Texas, Jeff became acquainted with a man by the name of John Turner. Jeff and John decided to leave for work at a lumber company in Alamogordo, New Mexico. However, after working in the company sawmill for a few months, Jeff decided he could make a lot more money by going into the mountains to cut logs for the sawmill. Grandma Jane and the children stayed in town while he worked in the mountains.

Shortly after the turn the century in 1900, Jeff quit the lumber business and moved his family back to Cliff New Mexico, where he bought a half-interest in a small cattle ranch. Taking his half of the cattle, Jeff moved the family fifteen miles up the Gila River from Cliff and started his own cattle ranch with his own brand. Finally, once again, Jeff began to prosper. In 1903 his cattle tally numbered 1,145, making him well-off financially by that day's standard. However, a severe drought began in late fall of 1903 and continued for the next two years forcing Jeff to sell half the herd to feed and cloth his family.

In the winter of 1905 the drought broke, only to be replaced by once-in-a-lifetime rains. The Gila River rose enough to wash away the family ranch destroying their crops and killing what was left of their cattle. The Powers moved back to Cliff. Charlie was now 15, Tom was 14 and John was 12 years of age. They all hired on as farm workers, freighters, blacksmiths and cowboys and did all they could to keep the family together.

In 1907 the Power family moved west close to the Arizona border where they had relatives. Jeff bought two small parcels of land totaling forty acres located in Doubtful Canyon area of southwestern New Mexico, within the rugged Horseshoe Mountains, where his brother-in-law Bill *"Wily"* Morgan was a successful cattle rancher. Spending two unsuccessful years there, Jeff sold the ranch at a loss but had saved enough money to allow him to purchase another ranch that was for sale in nearby Rattlesnake Canyon, which was located in the Galiuro Mountain range. With guidance from their Uncle *"Wily,"* a prosperous rancher in this Mormon community, was the brother of deceased Martha Morgan Power. Uncle Wily had personal knowledge of the ranch and told Jeff the ranch had great potential. He hoped this ranch would be their last move to a permanent ranch of their own and that with hard work he was confident the Power family could make a go out of the ranch.

Chapter Two

I paraphrase as Charlie Power picks up the story. It was a cold and damp morning as we prepared to leave our home in Doubtful Canyon. It had snowed off and on through the night and we woke to a two-inch layer of snow on the high desert which was covered by Juniper Pinion trees. The sun was shinning and the snow usually melted by noon. It was a glorious day and the whole family was looking forward to settling down in one place that we could finally call home after our nomadic life style, since our mother had passed away.

Uncle Bill (Wily) Morgan, our mother's brother talked our father into relocating to Arizona. Dad told us he bought a successful cattle ranch operation near the town of Klondyke, Arizona. Dad bought it site unseen. He wanted a permanent place that would allow us to be a family. Dad, Tom, John and I rounded up our cattle which numbered only about 150 along with six hogs and a coup full of chickens for the trail drive. Granny and Ola May, our little sister, packed the wagon. According to Uncle Wily it was about 150 miles from Doubtful Canyon to Klondyke, where he planned to meet and guide us to our new home. I'm guessing the distance estimated was a bit farther, as travelling by highways today the distance is nearly 140 miles. He had written a letter explaining he would meet us at the Klondyke store sometime on the 15th of February. We traveled nearly thirty-five miles that first day, making excellent time. We camped by a stream about four in the afternoon. The stream provided fresh water for us and all the animals. We pitched our 20 x 20 canvas army tent. There was plenty of room between our six sleeping bags and cots so we had no worries about bumping into one another if nature called during the night.

Dinner consisted of homemade biscuits, cowboy beans and dried beef jerky from a cow we had butchered before starting our trip. Granny and Ola May had stuffed a big gunny sack full of homemade buttermilk biscuits and corn dodgers, hard corn-based biscuits we also ate on trail.

It was a cold evening and we sat around the campfire after dinner drinking coffee and discussing our plans. We retired around eight snug and warm in the sleeping bags dad had given us for Christmas presents some years back. Early the next morning after breakfast we broke camp and continued our journey.

We traveled about 40 miles the second day, again setting up camp near a watering hole. However, the water was not clear and we did not drink it since we had two twenty-gallon-leather bags full of drinking water. We had filled them up at the last spring. However, the animals could drink from the watering hole.

The next 3 days were pretty uneventful, though we averaged almost thirty miles each day but the trip tried our patience and exhausted us all. We were able to stop and take a bath a couple of times. The water was ice cold as it was still February. But, water is water and one has to make due with the primitive conditions of a trail ride.

On the morning of the 14th we awoke after camping the night and gathered up the animals for another day on the trail. We ate a hardy breakfast and set forth. We only travelled about ten miles when we saw the Klondyke store on the horizon. It was quite a relief and welcome sight because we had arrived one day earlier than expected.

Riding up to the front of the store, we observed a man sitting in a rocking chair on the porch, smoking a pipe. I got off the wagon and said;

"Hello, my name is Charlie Power, who am I addressing?"

The gentleman stood up and stuck out his hand to shake mine and said;

"Lee Solomon, is my name."

Then he continued;

"It looks like you folks have come a long way. Where are you from?"

John told him that we had come from Doubtful Canyon in the New Mexico territory, and they were supposed to meet our Uncle Wily Morgan the next day here at the Klondyke Store. Wily was to guide us to a ranch our father purchased in a place called Rattlesnake Canyon which was supposed to be somewhere nearby.

Lee smiled and said, "I know "Wily" very well, but I call him Bill, and I know the ranch. He told me about you folks, and said he'd be here tomorrow. Then Lee suggested we stay in one his rental cabins or the one large bungalow, as we looked like we could use a good night's sleep.

Lee motioned that the rentals were just behind the store and that they should rent the bungalow, as it would be perfect for their whole family. Lee went on to say;

"It has four bedrooms with two beds in each room. It also has two bathrooms with two bathtubs and running water that is pumped from a well on the property and a gas heating system that would keep them warm through the cold night."

I agreed;

"We all need a bath, and it will be greatly appreciated by our family."

Then he asked Lee if there was anyplace to eat nearby? Lee told him there was a restaurant a short distance down the road that would provide them with a good dinner. He told us to settle in the bungalow and when we finished unpacking and we all got cleaned up, to meet him right here on the porch and we'd all go to dinner.

According to Lee Solomon, he told the owner of the store when he initially met the family;

> "The first time I saw the Power family ride up in front of the Klondyke store, I thought to myself that I had ever seen a stragglier looking bunch of folks in my life. Even the cattle looked mangy from their trip."

It took us about an hour to unload everything we needed for the night and to secure the rest of our belongings and get the livestock into corrals. After taking the longed-for warm baths and changing into clean clothes, we all met in the living room and walked the short distance to the front of the store. Lee was still sitting on the front porch smoking that same pipe and waiting patiently. I introduced Granny, Dad, my brothers John and Tom, and our little sister Ola May. After a little small talk, we walked down to the restaurant. Lee told us his first impressions of us were wrong. He had thought us to be a stubborn bunch of hard-nosed un-believers. However, he said he changed his mind about the family and grew to have great respect for our knowledge of livestock, our unbound tenacity and determination, and our love of family. Lee Solomon became a lifelong friend of both John and Tom Power. Lee mentioned to me later that evening, as we sat on the porch;

> "Now don't get upset, but those poor cattle looked like they had been to hell and back."

Tom smiled and said;

"Yes, I know. It was a long hard cold trip from Doubtful Canyon and the trip took a heavy toll on the animals. We're just glad it's about over that we are here now and are looking forward to seeing our new home."

Lee assured me the spread had great potential with the right family working the ranch and with a lot of hard work and perseverance we could make the ranch into one of the best in the Galiuro mountain range. He said the property was about 20 miles away, located in Rattlesnake Canyon and consisted of 300 acres of good grazing and another 500 acres of rough terrain, but it had plenty of foliage to feed their cattle and horses. He said that our family, along with the other ranchers in the area, had grazing rights to the two thousand acres of national forest land adjacent to their ranch. Lee went on to say the immediate property had two dwellings.

The Garden House which consisted of two acres already set up to grow crops, including a nice size corral to keep hogs. There was another structure near the Garden House that had been used by local ranchers as a saloon. In addition, there was a cabin near a mine located about five miles up in the Kielberg Canyon that belonged to their family and was being used by miners.

The next morning. we were greeted by uncle Wily who had come to guide us to the new ranch. We were so excited to finally see him. John said;

"Uncle, you're a sight for sore eyes."

Uncle Wily told us he brought along two of his top ranch hands, Travis and Todd, to help us drive our stock and the wagon with our belongings to our new home. Before breakfast that morning we stopped by the store and restocked with flour, sugar, salt and seed along with a case of whiskey. Then we met up with our new friend, Lee Solomon who walked with us to the restaurant. Preparing for the last leg of our journey we ate a big hearty breakfast. After eating and catching up on the local happenings we walked back to finish packing. Travis and Todd helped to hitch the wagon and round up the seventy-five cows, twenty horses and the five hogs. We loaded our chickens and started off. Lee joined us because he was familiar with the new ranch and would be a good guide, plus he was downright curious to see our reactions.

Below is a photo of the Klondyke store that was found in our National Archives, Circa 1900.

This is a photo taken by the author of the Klondyke Store as it appears today.

Chapter Three

The whole family was excited about the final 12 miles to get to their new home. They heard from Lee and their Uncle Will that it was a desolate but beautiful canyon. As they looked at the terrain, surrounding the store there was no way they could ever figure there was anything beautiful about the country. They all thought that it was almost as desolate and harsh as the ranch they left in Texas after the two-year drought. Lee noticed John, Tom and Charlie talking about the terrain. They asked him how cattle were able to live in such a desolate area. Lee just laughed and said they do just fine. He said there were plenty of water tanks in the area filled by windmill pumps along with several streams and that amazingly the cattle had plenty of foliage to eat. He explained their new ranch looked nothing like the area around the store. That was hard to believe.

Below is a photo taken by the author of the Aravapai Valley near the Klondyke Store

The party approached the mouth of Rattlesnake Canyon about 9 o'clock on the morning of February 15th 1909. They saw more Juniper trees, Barrel cactus, sage and Scrub Oak trees in the terrain, rather than the Mesquite trees, Cholla cactus and tumbleweeds they had seen on the ride from Doubtful Canyon and around Klondyke. The surroundings reminded them of their ranch in New Mexico. They were pleasantly surprised to see that the cattle would thrive in this country. Little did they know how much the terrain would change again over the next few miles.

Below is a photo taken by the author from the top of Rattlesnake Mesa. Notice how the shrubbery has changed from the terrain in and around Klondyke. The vegetation is mostly Bear Grass and cactus. The beginning of Rattlesnake Canyon can be seen in the middle of the picture.

The canyon was about 60 feet wide as they started in. They could see in the distance that it narrowed. It looked like the trail stopped completely about 2 miles into the canyon. Lee told them that it looked like it ended but that Rattlesnake Canyon was well named. He told them it winds around and narrows to ten feet wide in some locations but it opens up just as one gets to the Garden Cabin, at the west end of the ranch. They could hardly believe that the terrain could change so dramatically, especially when they were surrounded by the wild flowers and carpets of green, thick vegetation.

The so called trail, according to Charlie Power was very rough. They had to move several big rocks so their wagon could get through. They knew at some point a real road would have to be built along the trail to their ranch if they were going to have any success moving cattle to market. About 3 miles into the canyon, the trail narrowed to hardly twenty feet and winded north for about 100 yards then headed east again. The walls of the canyon were sheer rock and very steep. As they went through the turn they noticed water pouring from a spring in the rock wall about fifty feet up the face of the cliff. The water was streaming down the cliff and into a creek that ran east. The terrain in the canyon, on both sides of the creek, was filled with beautiful Elm and Ash trees some occasional Barrel Cactus and lots of wild lavender, sage and even wild rose bushes. It was well shaded by the steep high cliff walls and there was green foliage everywhere. The trail went right down the creek which was very sandy and not so rocky. It was much easier for us to herd our cattle and drive our wagon. We enjoyed the trip covering the next four miles even when the canyon narrowed to ten feet. We saw three more spring-fed waterfalls in the cliffs which widened the creek to about ten feet in some places and to a depth of five to seven feet. We were awestruck as the beautiful trail crossed back and forth over Rattlesnake Creek causing no travel problems.

The creek made one more turn north going about a hundred yards and then turned east again. Another small stream came from a narrow canyon which also flowed into Rattlesnake Creek. At that point the stream was running pretty strong and fifteen feet wide in some areas. We could see a cabin in a large clearing about a mile east with the creek running about two hundred yards in front of it. The cottage was covered with beautiful trees affording a lot of shade and there were several pastures surrounding the cottage. We exited into an opening some 500 yards wide, between the tall walls of the canyon; it was a remarkable place. Charlie said he remembered when the whole family got down from the wagon and just stood there staring at the steep canyons in the distance with the sun shinning off the water running in front of their beautiful new land;

> *"None of us said a word for about ten minutes as we all looked at Uncle Wily and Lee Solomon in silent amazement."*

Both men laughed and said;

> *"We told you so."*

it is simply amazing how much the terrain can change in this crazy Arizona Territory. Charlie recalled that dad and Grandma broke out in tears and hugged each other as they shared how Martha would have been so excited.

Dad held grandma and Uncle Will's hand and exclaimed out loud;

> *"Mary, we have arrived at the place you dreamed about and we know you are with us. It is as beautiful as you said it would be and a true paradise."*

At that point, John, Tom and I turned the cattle and horses loose to drink water and graze. They herded the four hogs into a pen on the east side of the building. A bit further east of that was a corral big enough for the four horses and the four mules.

> On the next page is a picture of the Power family spring near the Garden Cabin in Rattlesnake Canyon, that is

also used with permission from the Hiking.com website

While we unloaded the wagon Lee, Uncle Will, dad, grandma and Ola May took a walk around the cabin making assessments as to what needed to be fixed. The cabin had a large living area with a fireplace and a nice kitchen. On one side of the cabin was a bedroom for Ola May and grandma. There were two other smaller bedrooms on the west side of the cabin that would be for the boys and dad. These observations and room assignments were determined by grandma, who was as stubborn and hard headed as her son Jeff. However, dad never argued with his mother because as he told us boys laughingly;

"Whether she is right or wrong it is her way or the highway."

After our initial observations, Uncle Wily, his two ranch hands, Lee Solomon, dad, Tom, John and I (Charlie) sat on the front porch to smoke a cigarette. Dad broke out a carefully saved bottle of Jack Daniels for celebrating the move to our new home. Ola May and grandma were busy cleaning the cabin making it ready for the men to move in the furniture. The place had wood floors and there was a big bed frame in grandma and Ola May's room. There were two bed frames in each of the other two bedrooms. All the gals had to do was make mattresses for each of the frames. All in all, the place was actually in great condition. Uncle Wily told us the previous owners had only moved out about two months before. There were even vegetables growing in the garden ready for picking. Everyone loved our new home.

After the women finished, everyone pitched in to unload the furniture and all of the household items from the wagon. After giving us specific instructions as to where to place each piece of furniture, the women went into the kitchen and began making dinner. Tom, John and I gathered wood and started a fire in the fireplace in addition to the wood burning stove in the kitchen where the women began to cook dinner.

Below is a phot of the Power Garden Cabin that was Ola Mae Power residence, used with the permission from Hiking.com

Uncle Wily, Travis, Todd and Lee Solomon decided they had better begin heading back to Klondyke before dark. We invited the men to spend

the night but they said they had things to do and needed to get home so they could be ready for work the next day. They stuck around for another hour and ate dinner with us though. Dinner consisted of a pot roast, purchased back at the Klondyke store, along with potatoes and carrots, plus some fresh baked biscuits. Ola May had picked some wild sage, rosemary and basil from the garden which they threw in the pot to flavor the meat and vegetables. After dinner the men sat on the porch and shared some more Jack Daniels. A short time later, Uncle Wily, Lee, and the ranch hands said goodbye and left for Klondyke. Lee Solomon figured the last five miles would be in the dark but he knew the trail like the back of his hand and told us they should have no problems. Lee assured them that he would visit the ranch the following week to see if they had any questions or problems after they had settled in.

The picture above was taken supplied with permission of the hiking.com website. It is a trail about a quarter of a mile from the Power Garden Cabin Ranch showing the trail that Lee, Uncle Wily and the boys took back to Klondyke. Rattlesnake

Creek is dry at this point. Beyond the trees at the rear is where one of the springs fed the creek. It starts to run again from there by the Garden Cabin and continues beyond the Mine Cabin, not an unusual phenomenon in Arizona. Lots of creeks and rivers run below ground, surface and then return below ground. The Apaches figured out that if one digs down in the dry areas along a creek bed that often clean pristine water will bubble up to the surface.

Chapter Four

The next morning after breakfast, Dad, John, Tom and Charlie took a ride to find the other cabin. Lee told them the cabin was located about two miles or so east of the Garden Cabin straight up the canyon trail. He said it was near a gold mine that was also located on their property but the mineral rights to the mine were owned by several people. Lee told them as long as they introduced themselves as the new ranch owners all would be fine. Lee said the two miners were as different as night and day; they were always arguing and fighting but they were good men and would be easy to get along with.

A picture of the Power Mine Cabin taken by the author on his visit to the gunfight site and is being used for the cover of this book.

As we approached the mine, we saw the cabin and could hear and see the two men bickering in the distance. One of the miners went into the mine shaft and the other one came out to meet us. He had a pistol in his hand and pointed it at us boys and asked who we were and what our business was at the mine. We gave him our names and explained we were the sons of the new ranch owner. The man put his gun in his pants and introduced himself as C. P. Talbot and said his partner working in the mine was named John Bauman. C. P. went on to say that he owned a quarter interest in the mine along with an investor, R. C. Elton and that Bauman owned a half interest in the mine. He said that he and Bauman lived in the nearby cabin. He then proceeded to take us on a tour of the property and showed us the cabin they had built. He said even though they lived and worked the mine together, often they disagreed with each other.

The entrance to the Power gold mine. This photo was found in our National Archives.

As C.P was showing us around his partner John came out of the mine with a load of ore. Seeing us, Mr. Bauman shouted,

"Who the hell are you guys?"

C.P took us over and introduced us to his partner. John was actually very gracious after he found out we were the new owners of the ranch. John explained they had been working the mine for over a year and had been taking out a low grade of gold but he said he just hit a vein and now hoped their hard work would finally pay off. He went on to say that they needed to get a boiler and stamp mill up to the mine so they could really start processing larger levels of ore since finally hitting a great gold vein. He said the ore from their mine consisted of gold, silver and mercury, and up to now the value of the mercury was more than the gold and silver. He took the three boys back into the mine where they saw the gold vein with their own eyes. It looked to be a huge one two feet wide and two feet high, carrying down the side of the shaft. There was no doubt they had hit a major vein. They made the boys swear an oath to keep it a secret. Charlie said they all took the oath and promised not to tell. After that the boys asked the miners that if for some reason an interest in the mine ownership came up, they would be interested in buying the share and were also willing to work the mine.

They all went into the cabin, sat down and had a cup of coffee. They conversed for about a half hour. C.P and Bauman seemed to get along while they were there visiting. Each repeated the oath to say nothing about the gold discovery. Everyone was quite excited after seeing the vein of gold. Finishing their cups of coffee, the boys said goodbye and told them that if they needed any help their cabin was only a couple miles down the trail. They couldn't wait to get back and tell their father about the mine and their friends.

The boys arrived back at their cabin just before dark. Dad, Ola May and Grandma were working in the garden, preparing it for more planting. Their father inquired if they found the mine. The boys told him they did and that they met the owners. They asked their dad to come inside to discuss the mine, the owners and especially the possibility of becoming part owners of the mine if they were just patient. They explained the mine had great potential and they had hit it off well with the two owners. However, Jeff opened the conversation by saying;

> *"Boys I know you mean well but in fact, we just arrived at our new home and we have a lot of work ahead of us to cultivate the land, grow crops, raise livestock and I really do not think we can branch out into mining right now."*

He went on to say,

> *"I'd be open to what you think, but we must take into consideration that mining is hard work and again right now we have a lot of hard work to get the ranch in a position to start repaying our investment."*

After our brief talk dad wanted an exacting description of the mine property including the cabin and what we learned about the miners. We told dad the mine had three partners. One partner, C.P. Talbot, working the mine, owned a quarter-interest. John Bauman, his working partner had a half interest. We said another quarter interest in the mine was owned by a non-working investor, R.C. Elton.

> *"We believe Talbot is jealous of Bauman who holds the half interest."*

Talbot said they didn't like the fact they were doing all the hard work and had to split the take with a non-working investor. We told dad there was bad blood between the two shareholders and that we actually heard them arguing and saw them fighting. Things seemed as though they would only get worse as the mining progressed dad's only comment was;

> *"Again, I think we need to concentrate on building our ranch, but we will keep our options open."*

Over the next two years we worked very hard to build our ranch up and increase our cow and calf numbers to 350 and expand our horse count from 20 to 50. Our efforts had paid off and we brought our investments into profitability. Grandma Jane and Ola May had been quite successful growing crops and we were finally in a position to feed ourselves from the land and sell extra produce as well.

We converted the saloon building into a storage bin for the harvested crops and sectioned a portion off to preserve our dried meats to get us through the winters.

The photo above was taken by hiking.com and used with their permission and is of the barn and saloon at the Garden Cabin. The Saloon, on the right, was converted to a cold storage building. The barn was used to store mining equipment.

It was sometime early on morning on March 10th 1911. C.P Talbot, one of the owners of the mine came by our ranch and seemed very upset. We three boys were working in the garden when we saw him ride up. Dad invited him in for coffee. C.P. told dad that he and Bauman his partner had a huge fight. He asked if we would be interested in buying the other quarter interest in the mine that was owned by the investor R. C. Elton who lived in Miami, Arizona. Talbot pointed out that Elton owned a lot of claims in the area and wanted to sell out his interest in their mine. He said Bauman forbid C.P. from buying the share so they had a big fight that nearly resulted a gunfight. Dad asked C.P.;

"How much does Elton want for the quarter share in the mine?"

C.P said he wanted $2,500. Father said that we did not have that kind of money on hand but wanted talk over the possibility of the investment with us boys before making a final decision.

After talking with dad, Talbot left that morning on his way to Miami to meet with Mr. Elton. Father talked it over with us boys and we all decided the ranch was doing well enough that he and our new hired hand would continue to work the ranch and that we three boys could help with the mining venture if Talbot came back from Miami with the okay to sell Elton's portion of the mine to us.

Two days later again early in the morning, Talbot returned. We all gathered outside the cabin when he rode up, anxious to hear what he had to say. He told us;

"I talked with Mr. Elton and he told me to relay his wishes to sell his one quarter interest in the mine to you for $2,500 dollars."

Talbot told us the deal would be finalized and we would own the quarter interest when we paid Elton the money. Right after Talbot left, my father said;

"Ok boys go ahead and pick out twenty-five head of horses and we will

take them to the Wilcox bank and sell them to get the money to buy the mine interest."

We were all very excited. We could hardly believe the day finally came that would give us the opportunity to work the mine that was there on our property. We selected twenty-five horses and picked up dad as we went by the cabin. He had packed lunch and had a large leather bag full of water for the trip. We herded the horses down the trail, stopped at a water hole and rode about seven miles that day. There was plenty of grass to feed our horses and also plenty of water for them to drink. We pitched camp, built a fire, had a bite to eat, and were preparing to hit the sack. We planned an early start the next morning. Just as we were ready to retire, we heard someone rather noisily approaching our camp fire. Two men came into camp;

"Good evening, welcome to our camp. Come on over by the fire and get warm." dad said. We could see over the dimly lit fire that it looked like John Bauman, but we did not recognize the other man. Dad asked, "Is that you, Mr. Bauman?"

The man answered yes and introduced the other man as Lee Kemper the local forest ranger;

"You're pretty close to home aren't you Mr. Power?"

Ranger Kemper spoke in a shaky voice;

"I don't know about that, answered our father."

Right away they said they needed to be on their way and thanked us for our hospitality. What a strange encounter. We had heard Bauman and Talbot were known to kill deer out of season now and then so we thought Ranger Kemper may have caught Bauman

poaching. We though that explained Bauman's shaky voice and why the two
did not stop, get warm, and visit with us for a bit.

In the early morning after breakfast we headed the horses toward Klondyke, and soon ran into Ron Walton, a justice of the peace, with a group of men. Justice Walton told us the men were a coroner's jury and they were just returning from a murder scene at the mine. It was common practice for the jury members to visit crime scenes in those days. He said Kemper killed C.P. Talbot the evening before. No wonder Kemper and Bauman acted so unusual last night. Wooten explained;

> "Kemper had called Talbot out, accusing him of making insulting remarks about a woman."

A posse had taken Kemper into custody for shooting and killing Talbot, but strangely enough we later found the coroner's jury brought no charges against Kemper.

We quit moving the horses after the conversation our father had with Justice Walton. Dad told us boys that since Talbot was dead we had to wait until his estate was settled before we could invest in the mine. We boys were disappointed but me (Charlie) and my younger brothers Tom and John understood our father's logic, not to get mixed up in a big mess with Talbot's heirs, so we took the horses back to our ranch.

Two days later, dad and Tom went to Wilcox to buy supplies, but they did not go to the bank to get a loan to buy Talbot's interest in the mine at that time, deciding to wait until the messy estate was
settled.

Chapter Five

In the summer of 1912 the Walsh brothers, two large cattle ranchers from Globe came to our place and told us they had purchased 67 brands of cattle and that some of the cattle were grazing in our area as well as the neighboring Redfield and Aravaipai Canyons. We agreed to go to work for them to help gather up their cattle. We were paid $40 a month each and were allowed to work our own cattle. It was a good deal for me and my brothers. Dad, Grandma and Ola May took care of our ranch and crops.

After the roundup the Walsh brothers had us come to Globe to help them and their friends the Gibson brother's roundup more cattle from several other ranches whose brand they also bought. We spent over a month in and around Globe and rounded up some 1,700 cows, steers and calves for them. We separated each animal according to its brand and kept them in separate corrals so the Walsh brothers and the Gibson's could get an idea which brands were worth keeping and which ones they would sell off. Some of the cattle with different brands looked healthier than others and that was how they would make their final determination. The cattle were kept in those corrals for two months while they were fed well to fatten them up for market. When the cattle come off the range they are full grown but generally pretty mangy. It takes two to three months of being fed corn and other grains to fill them out so they are ready for market.

Charlie said, he and his brothers stayed in Globe after the roundup and worked odd jobs. They worked for two local grain store suppliers feeding cattle and loading grain and feed into customer's trucks. They hired on with a freighter and did mechanic work on all of the store's trucks, mainly changing the oil and filters.

We bought a seven passenger Hudson that was worn out from driving the rough roads. We overhauled the motor ourselves. While we were working around Globe, I ran into Jim Anderson, a friend, we knew from New Mexico. The night we finished working on the car, Jim's wife invited us to come to dinner. After we finished our supper Jim asked;

> "How'd you boys like a drink of whiskey?"

Tom and John said;

> "Fine"

Jim reached up on top of a kitchen cupboard and brought down a quart of whiskey. My brothers, Jim, and I finished that quart of whiskey as we sat on the porch talking and catching up on Jim's life. As we were ready to leave my brother Tom told Jim that he would give him $20 for a quart of whiskey so we could it take home to our father. Jim told us he knew a guy who might have some whiskey to sell. He gave us the man's name and address. Jim called the man to tell him we were coming. He gave us a bottle and it didn't cost us a cent.

It is necessary to understand that our Arizona Territorial Governor, Hunt, adopted prohibition in 1909 along with eighteen other states. He also abolished the death penalty and closed down the Yuma Territorial prison due to the inhumane practices that existed. He had a new state prison built in Florence, AZ, where it still stands today. His plan was to show the politicians in Washington that we were no longer a wild territory known for lynch mobs and hangings for major crimes and that we were ready for statehood. There were a total of eighteen states that had adopted prohibition. Those states set the precedent that forced the politicians in Washington to adopt the 1919 Volstead Act, which made it a federal offense to transport or drink liquor. However, adopting prohibition opened the door to a new industry, called bootlegging. It was an illegal business involved in distilling, selling, and transporting whiskey, beer and wine. All sorts of people in our state were involved in the bootlegging industry in many forms.

After that night my brother Tom started selling whiskey under the protection of U.S. District Deputy Marshal Frank Haynes, the Sheriff of Gila County. Our friend Jim set Tom up in business with the sheriff's office and the Globe City, Chief of Police. John and I went back to our ranch. We did not want any part of any unlawful shenanigans, even though we would be under the protection of the two most powerful law officers in the state. Even more unusual was the fact that these operations were taking place in a predominately Mormon community.

Bother Tom went down to the Globe Chief of Police and talked to him privately. The chief asked Tom, "What is your line of business?" Tom told him that his partner was Jim Anderson and they wanted to sell whiskey. The chief and Tom went into a back room. There was a card table with chairs all around the room and around the table. A man stepped through the back door of the room. The chief held up two fingers. The man standing in the door brought a bottle of whiskey and two glasses put them on the card table then left the room, leaving Tom with the chief. The chief poured a drink for himself and my brother. They drank another shot and the chief asked Tom;

> "What do you think of the quality of this liquor?"

Tom Power speaks up saying;
> "It tastes good, but not as good as the hooch Jim Anderson gets from his source."

My brother had two pints in each of his coat pockets. He took out one of the pints and poured a shot for himself and the chief. The chief asked;

> *"Is that the whiskey you're going to sell?"*

Tom said it was.

> *"O.K, it's definitely good quality hooch, but keep the bottles in your coat pockets so my boys won't see them."*

Jim Anderson and my brother Tom officially went into the bootlegging business. They had two Model T Fords, plus the second-hand Hudson. One of Jim Anderson's brothers was married and living in El Paso. He was not doing so well. Jim and Tom sent for him and let him have one of the Fords. He went into the bootlegging business with Jim and Tom. They started hauling whiskey from Lordsburg, New Mexico to Safford and Globe. They made seven trips. On the seventh trip, carrying an obvious full load with cases of whiskey, they reached Cutter, which used to be a railroad station south of Globe. Here they met Deputy Marshal Haynes and a carload of deputies. They blew their horn and waved hello as they passed the officers the road. A little farther on, they met another car that was full of law officers and then a third car with more law officers on the road headed for San Carlos. Jim and Tom were very happy that they were in business with the sheriff and head of the police department or there would have been hell to pay.

Tom stopped buying whiskey in Lordsburg, and began buying from another bootlegger from Globe which was quite a bit closer to Safford. Often Jim and Tom would frequent the sheriff's office and drink with him and his deputies. They would also go over to the county attorney's office and *"get loaded."* Tom had all the law officers around Globe, even the motorcycle officers on their side.

There became too much competition in the area so Tom and Jim quit the bootlegging whiskey business, but they kept the great relationships they had enjoyed with the Globe, Safford, Gila County, Graham County officers and the U.S. Marshals

Tom worked around Globe and Superior for different cattle ranches and gold mines during the next two years; he returned home to our ranch in Rattlesnake Canyon in 1915. He learned a lot about gold mining over the two years he was gone. Tom got restless working on our ranch and liked to takeoff checking out other opportunities. Before he and my brother John would leave they would make sure that all was well with the stock and crops then they would tell the family they need to so their wild oats.

The first trouble we had with the Wooten family, was when we caught them roping and driving our cattle off the forest reserve. We had a permit that allowed our stock to graze from the north boundary of nearby Aravaipai Canyon a canyon just north of Rattlesnake Canyon to the drift fence of Redfield Canyon which was adjacent to Rattlesnake Canyon to the south. Tom, John and I caught two of the Wooten brothers rounding up our cattle on Squaw Creek. We warned them not to rope our stock, holding them at gunpoint while we cut out our stock.

They told us to meet them outside the Klondyke store the next morning for a talk. At the time Bill Wooten owned a 30/30 carbine, Frank Wooten had a 44/30 single action Colt pistol and Thomas (aka; T.K.) Wooten carried a .30 caliber German Luger. We agreed to meet the Wooten brothers in front of the Klondyke store the following morning. However, when we met them the next morning, not one of them was carrying a gun. We all went inside after a little small talk and had breakfast and discussed our chores for the day. Not one word was said about the incident that took place the day before. We got along with the Wooten family for the most part, except the times when we were working our cattle and horses. Harsh words were exchanged between us, but that was as far as it went.

Later that year our older brother Charles sold his share of the cattle to us and moved back to Cliff, New Mexico, never to return. He told us he had enough of the rough, primitive and uncertain life we led, and wanted to make a new life. He told us our uncle Ben owned a general store in Cliff and an opening came up for him to run the store for their uncle. We never heard from him again. Charles's leaving took a heavy toll on all of us.

About the same time Charlie left, Jay Mahoney, a neighbor who had a small mining claim about a mile above us up Rattlesnake Canyon, was stealing cattle, making jerky, then selling it to Fort Thomas. Graham County Deputy Sheriff Frank McBride caught Mahoney on the road headed to Fort Thomas packed to the gills with beef jerky. Mahoney told the sheriff that we gave it to him.

The sheriff took Mahoney's word, and later, in cahoots with T. K. (aka; Kane) Wooten, issued a warrant for our arrest for stealing cattle. When we ran into Deputy Sheriff Frank McBride later that month, he did not arrest us. He asked us about the beef jerky incident and we told him we caught Mahoney stealing cattle with the Wooten brand, near his mining claim just north of our cabin in Rattlesnake Canyon. Deputy McBride told us he had an idea that Mahoney was the thief. He knew us personally and knew that we would never be involved in stealing cattle, making beef jerky and selling it to the army. Nothing else was ever said about the incident and the warrant was never served on us.

In early January of 1916, C.P Talbot's estate was finally settled. My father closed the deal to buy Mr. Elwood's interest in the gold mine that we almost purchased two years earlier but were afraid to close the deal due to Talbot's death. After closing the deal with Mr. Elwood for the original $2,500 price that was agreed upon; we owned a quarter interest in the mine.

Two men, Harry Beal and Ed Miller, owned a quarter interest in the mine, and Al Bauman owned the other quarter interest in the mine. Our family and the three other owners started doing assessment work at the mine. We were offering a ten per cent commission to anyone who could sell the property for a minimum of $100,000. The Inspiration Copper Company was interested in purchasing our mine. They sent an engineer by the name of Ken Grimes to buy the mine. He agreed to buy the property for the $100,000 asking price but the company wanted to pay us in monthly installments over the next two years. Beal wanted 20 per cent down, but Grimes said Inspiration would not agree to pay a large down payment. Instead he offered not to take the ten percent commission and for us to use that as the down payment. Beal told him;

> *"Before he would agree to take less than 20 per cent down, he would rather let the gold lie there and let the bugs eat it."*

Grimes offered us all good paying jobs if we would sell the mine to Inspiration. He said they knew we were good workers and they needed folks to work the mine. Beal would still not accept Grimes' offer. Beal and Miller began quarreling. Beal carried a rifle and Miller was armed with a double barrel shotgun. He said Jeff told them;

> *"A killing would help solve the problem but only make it more complex with one or both dead and the rest of*

us having again to wait until estates were settled."

Beal and Miller lived in the cabin at the mine. We were unable to close a deal with Grimes and The Inspiration Copper Company so we all left leaving Beal and Miller to work the mine and hopefully not kill each other. We went back to working our cattle. It wasn't until several years later that we sold our cattle, and again made preparations to start working the mine.

It was in June of 1917. We received a letter from Mr. Elwood informing us that Bauman wanted to sell his half interest in the mine. My brother John and I went to Globe, while I competed in a rodeo, John went through a blinding snow storm to a mine on the Black River to meet Bauman. John brought him back to Globe and we finalized the deal to buy his half interest in the mine. That gave the Power family three-quarter interest in the mine, which was composed of five claims. I already owned four mining claims on Gold Mountain and John had the extensions on both ends of the abandoned claim. We also had two claims at Rattlesnake Spring ranch and two more claims at Mills Camp.

We realized that we needed a stamp mill and boiler in order to process larger amounts of ore. The Arastra we had been using was simply too time consuming and we could not process enough ore to make it worth our while. The big problem facing us was to transport the stamp mill and boiler through rattlesnake canyon to the mine. The road from Klondyke to Rattlesnake Canyon was fine, but from the mouth of Rattlesnake Canyon to the mine that was the problem. We started building the road in the fall of 1917.

A man came by the Mine Cabin one morning looking for work. His name was "Big" Tom Sisson. He hit it right off with the Power family. He told them he was broke, dispirited and at their first impression, he looked like he was no stranger to hard work. He told Jeff he had recently been released from the Arizona State Prison where he spent one year for being a horse thief which he told us was a trumped up charge. A chance for a bed, food, clothing and tobacco with a provision of cash when the mine started paying was just what the doctor ordered in his current condition in life.

Sisson was open to tell the Power men that he had a troubled childhood. He was happy to be free again. The ex-convict talked freely to the Power men. He told them he was born in Minnesota in 1869. There were too many children in the household for their father to feed and cloth so Big Tom left home early. By the time he was sixteen years old he had been away from home for over two years. He told Jeff and the boys that he finally went back home but nobody noticed or seemed to care so he departed never to return. He spent time working on the Mississippi working as a freighter then he did spend fifteen years in the United States Army and that his last eight years was spent at Fort Grant as a scout. He said he was familiar with the area because he was involved in the capture of Geronimo and was involved in hunting the renegade Apache Kid.

He was discharged from the Army in 1896 and remained in the Fort Grant-Wilcox area working for different ranches in the Aravaipa Valley. He was illiterate but that was not a problem for a man with his rough influence and was a perfect match for the Power family men who were also rough, hard working men.

So, Tom Sisson was willing to assume his load of the heavy labor in helping construct the road. He appeared enthusiastic about the project and was an inspiration to the Power men during construction.

The photo on the next page of an Arastra, just like the one the Power brothers used, was taken by the author outside a restaurant in Superior. The arastra was used to crush raw ore and was pulled by a mule or a horse. One can see that it was not a very efficient method

We had a great road construction crew consisting of me, my brother John, Dad and Tom Sisson; once in a while we would hire our neighbor Jeff Clanton to help us move boulders. My sister Ola May and Grandma Jane would make us lunch each day. We had a buckboard that was pulled by single horse or mule they used to bring us lunch and water everyday. On the morning of September 16th 1917, Ola was not able to find a horse or mule; all the stock was out of the corrals and grazing in nearby Aravaipa Canyon. Our neighbor Jeff Clanton lent them a horse to use to hookup to the   wagon. The horse had just been broken and was wild. Ola said they were about a mile from where we were working, and that the horse got spooked when it saw a rattlesnake and took off on a dead run. Ola walked to where we were working to tell us that she could not slow down the darn horse. She explained they hit a boulder in the road and it wrecked the wagon, and the borrowed horse ran off. She said her and grandma both went airborne. She, catching her breath, said she had landed on her back and that her neck and back were in a lot of pain. She sadly told us grandma hit her head on a rock when she landed and died instantly of the severe head injury.

Dad took Ola to Doc Warner in Safford several times over the next six months to be treated for her neck and back injuries from the accident. The Doc told dad she had a herniated a disc in her neck and one in her upper back. He said with rest and the exercises he gave her to do that she would eventually recover. He said she would always have a weakness in those areas and might have to live with pain for a long time. He gave her pain pills, a neck collar and told her to rest her neck and return in a month. Of course, Ola being the strong willed gal that she was, kept the collar on for about a week, then it was thrown in the corner of the cabin where she lived. She did take the pain meds and exercised as Doc Warner's had instructed. She complained from time to time, when she over worked but the pain never kept her down.

We transported grandma's body to a church in Klondyke where we had a funeral then we buried her in the graveyard near the Klondyke store. I think it was it was September 18th 1917. Dad leased the improvements on our land at Rattlesnake Spring to Jeff Clanton. The lease included the home, the corrals, our windmill and the pasture fences. We still maintained ownership of the property. As part of the lease, we were allowed to store our mining equipment in the barn, until we had finished the road, then we would be allowed to move the equipment to our mine.

About two weeks after we signed the lease Mr. Sisson and my brother John moved the mining equipment from the barn at to Mr. Haby's place which was right up the road about a quarter of a mile from the Rattlesnake Spring property. His property was right on the road and it would make it easier to start to transport the equipment. Old man Clanton had Mr. Sisson and John arrested for stealing the mine equipment. How pathetic as it was this was the same horse caused Grandma Jane's death, for which he never apologized. Tom and John went to court and after showing the judge the lease with the clause that allowed us to keep the mining equipment on our property and proving that Clanton was only leasing the improvements the judge awarded $750 in damages to John and Mr. Sisson. I don't think they ever collected the $750 but at least old man Clanton never bothered us again.

While we were walking out of the Justice Court in Safford, after the judge had rendered his decision, we ran into Tom Algers, who was the Sheriff of Graham County, while we were walking out of the courtroom. My father introduced himself, Mr. Sisson my brother John and me, then he asked the sheriff;

"What's the good word?"

The sheriff told dad that he had heard there was rumor of some shootings around Klondyke and that he was headed over to check out who was making the *"pot shots."* I remember dad telling Algers that he was headed for trouble if he was going anywhere near Rattlesnake Canyon. He told the sheriff there were a lot of hard working ranchers and miners in the area and that if trouble started it would be the fault of the Wooten family, who were the singular instigators in the area. Dad went on to say;

> *"Other than the Wooten family everyone else in Rattlesnake Canyon and around Klondyke got along just fine."*

Dad reminded Algers to look elsewhere cause if he was going to Rattlesnake Canyon he was headed in the wrong direction. Sheriff Tom Algers took one look at dad, Mr. Sisson, John, and me and just tipped his hat in respect; he mounted his horse and rode away not saying a word.

A couple of weeks later, my brother John and I were on our way to Klondyke for supplies. We were about 200 yards north of the store when we rode up on Frank McBride in a sand wash. McBride was Sheriff Tom Algers chief deputy. Frank told us that he had just been fired by the sheriff, when Algers found out that he was planning on running against him also on the Democratic ticket in the upcoming election for sheriff.

We did not like Sheriff Algers, because of an accusation he made to our father about going into to Klondyke to take some pot shots. We figured the Wooten brothers were behind any shenanigans and that Algers was probably in cahoots with the them. We had some dealings with Deputy Sheriff Frank McBride over the years and we knew he was a good honest man with the right intentions for the county. We told him we would campaign for him. He said he wasn't worried about the county, that he just needed four precincts, the two at Klondyke and the two at Bonita. The day we talked to McBride at the sand wash, he told us he wanted me to be his under-sheriff if he was elected. I told him I did not want the job.

There was no kind of entertainment for people in the area to get together. So the first event we planned to raise money for McBride's campaign was to put on a free, roast-beef barbecue about a mile and a half from the Klondyke store. We picked a place that had a lot of shade trees, including cottonwoods, willows and mesquite. It had a beautiful stream of water running by the north side of the place and a big clearing that looked like a prairie withal the wild grass growing on it. We served lemonade to quench everyone's thirst.

Sam Martin and Bob Wooten corralled 30 head of wild burros. After dinner, we had a small rodeo, even though unsanctioned rodeos had been outlawed by the federal government in 1906. John and Tom collected $5 from each entrant to raise money for the campaign. We told them the overall winning cowboy would split the pot. The first event was goat roping. After that we proceeded to rope the wild burros that Bob and Sam Wooten had corralled. This was followed by saddling wild horses and we finished the rodeo with a horse race. The overall winner was Bob Wooten. He was a great overall cowboy and we raised almost $200 for Frank McBride's campaign.

Later that month, my brother John and I put on a picnic dinner and a free dance to campaign for McBride. All of the top politicians in the county came, among them was the county recorder, the judge and the county attorney. The whole slate we campaigned for was elected. We did not lose a single candidate. We carried all of the precincts, as well as the two in Klondyke and the two in Bonita that McBride needed. We didn't lose but two or three votes in those four precincts.

Newly elected Graham County Sheriff Frank McBride was as near a native Arizonan as possible. He was born in Eden, Utah on January 4th 1875 of Scottish decent. Frank's family emigrated from Utah to Safford, Arizona in 1876, when Frank was just a year old. His youth was spent laboring on the farm which helped him develop a dislike for farming. He took to being a cowboy and ranching. His love for horses made him a top hand. He became well acquainted with the vast valleys and mountain ranges of Eastern Arizona. He married Clara Sims in August of 1899. When questioned by a friend which one of the Sims gals he married his answer was;

"The prettiest one, of course."

He was a jolly, outgoing and happy man with a great personality and a great sense of humor. He was always in demand at parties and social events and was especially adept at writing short verses created on the spot for the entertainment of his friends. It was said of McBride that he had a profound respect for people, a virtue which accounted for his wide reputation as a man of his word. He was of high moral character, energetic, forceful and a good fighter when fighting was unavoidable. He was careful, deliberate and was as quick as a cat. He was never one to back down when the odds were great. General opinion of Sheriff McBride was that he was a man who would not leave his companions whether they were right or wrong. He was a lawman who admired Wyatt Earp. He was known to barge into situations that made him catch his breath. Several armed men would be involved, but cool words and straight looks, with no show of fear would do the job. He seemed to always have command of the situation.

In January 1915 he had been appointed to the office of chief deputy sheriff of Graham County serving under Tom Alger. The following year was when he ran for sheriff. His campaign manager was Tom Power. Frank McBride officially took office of the sheriff of Graham County, AZ., in January of 1917.

About a month after Frank was elected, John and I ran into Frank again outside the Klondyke store, when we were getting supplies. Frank talked to us for two hours in the store. He asked me to be his under-sheriff again. I told him I was still not interested. He told us there were lots of things going on in the sheriff's office that he knew I would not want to be a part of, but that I could run the office, drink good whiskey, smoke good cigars and prop my feet up on the desk. I still refused. Frank told us then that he knew there was a lot of cattle rustling happening and he hoped we might help know the suspects, since we lived here.

It was so ironic that we were talking about the cattle rustling, when Jay Mahoney came into the store and joined in our conversation. It took all John and I had to not tell the sheriff that we suspected the culprit that had just joined our conversation as the man who was doing the cattle rustling.

Chapter Six

World War One began in Europe in 1914. One of the main events that triggered our involvement took place in 1915. An American Cruise Ship, the Lusitania was attacked by a German submarine that took the lives of a 120 innocent people. A week later an English cruise ship, the Sussex was also attacked and sunk by another German submarine causing the deaths of even more innocent folks.

President, Teddy Roosevelt, was enraged and wanted revenge. But the United States did not enter the war until April 6th 1917. We lost no time producing many more propaganda posters than any other nation. They included recruitment to various services plus, the hugely successful Liberty Bond Issues were established to finance the war.

Three of the Author's favorite World War 1 posters

Due to the need to temporarily increase the military establishment here in the USA, the government passed the Selective Service Act on May 18th 1917. The Select Service system was initiated to select men for induction into the armed forces, progressing from the initial registration to the actual delivery of men to various military training camps.

Under the office of the Provost Marshal General, the Selective Service System was made up of 52 state offices *(one for each of the 48 states; the territories of Alaska, Hawaii, and Puerto Rico; and the District of Columbia)*, 155 district boards, and 4648 local boards. These organizations were responsible for registering men, classifying them, considering needs for manpower in certain industries and agriculture, as well as family situations of the registrants; handling appeals of these classifications; determining the medical fitness of individual registrants; determining the order in which registrants would be called; calling registrants; and placing them on trains to training centers. District boards were established by the President *(one or more for each Federal Judicial District)*. The average district board had jurisdiction over approximately 30 local boards, each with an average registration of 5,000 men. Local boards were established for each county or similar state subdivision.

There were three registration dates established during World War I;

1. The first, on June 5, 1917, was for all men between the ages of 21 and 31.
2. The second, on June 5, 1918, registered those who attained age 21 after June 5, 1917. *(A supplemental registration was held on August 24, 1918 for those becoming 21 years old after June 5, 1918. This was included in the second registration.)*
3. The third registration was held on September 12, 1918 for men aged 18 through 45.

At each of the three registrations, a different form was used, with a slight variation of questions asked. All three registrations included, full name, home address, exact date of birth, age in years, occupation, name and address of employer, citizenship status, citizen of what country, race, eye color, hair color, height, build, city/county and state of the local draft board, date of registration, and signature of applicant *(some in Yiddish)*!

At the first registration, the following additional information was recorded: exact birthplace, dependents, marital status, previous military service, and grounds for exemption. At the second registration, the following were also recorded: exact birthplace, nearest relative and address, and father's birthplace. At the third registration, for men aged 18-21 and 31-45 *(born between September 13, 1873 and September 12, 1900)*, the name and address of nearest relative were also recorded. Although the 2nd and 3rd drafts ask for name and address of nearest relative, they don't specify what their relationship. Note that the third registration did not request birthplace. If a male that fit the criteria and did not register, he was called, *"A Slacker."* A federal warrant was established for the arrest of any man that qualified and did not register. The penalty for not registering was a possible six-week sentence and small fine. It be noted that, state and county had a defined quota of men according to the population of that district, county or state.

The US district attorney has the final say if the slacker is indicted. However, since we had such a small population Tom and John were never notified by the forest service to come in to register. The real probability would have been that they would never have been indicted since the state quota was full. Typically, only 1 in 20 men that registered for the draft were actually called to fill our Territorial quota. Also taken into consideration would have been the fact that family hardship would play a part, their family relied on John and Tom to work the ranch, the mine and help provide for the family. Due to hardship they probably would never have been called to serve.

We were all working on the stamp mill, as it was still not operational, on June 23rd, 1917 when dad arrived back from taking Ola for another appointment with Doc Warner in Safford, to see if he could do anything for the pain she was having in her neck and back. He brought back an eight-day old newspaper indicating the first day to register for the draft for World War 1 was June 15th 1917.

John and I went down to the Post Office at Redington to pick up our mail and also to see what we needed to do to register for the draft. Dad was upset with us because we were going to register. He said we had just got started working the mine and that if we left it would only be him and Tom Sisson to do the work. He pleaded with us to just let it go. John and I did not want to break any laws and we read that the government would consider any family hardships before they drafted any men for active duty, so we decided it would be best to register.

On the following page is a newspaper article that appeared in the Arizona Republic on February 11th 1918. It bears out the Power brother's statement that Art Chambers told them when the brothers went to the Post Office to inquire about the World War One Selective Service Draft. It was a fact that the Arizona Draft was nearly full. Also Art Chambers, the Postmaster at the Redington Post Office doubled as the mailman and the government representative in the area. It also bears out the fact that he told the boys to go home and if they were needed the forest service would get a hold of them. The forest service had men in the field that doubled as forest rangers and federal representatives.

The postmasters at that time did not go in the field. The forest service was used as an extension of the post office if emergency mail had to be delivered. There was no actual mail delivery in those days as we have mail carriers today. One has to keep in mind we were still a young state having becoming a state just six years earlier. on February 12th 1918. Arizona had a small, mostly rural population in those days, as is still is today. Most of our population in Arizona was in Maricopa and Pima Counties, which included the cities of Phoenix and Tucson. Below is an article published in the Tucson Daily Star newspaper;

Arizona Draft Quota Nearly Complete

Phoenix, Feb. 11--- Arizona men will not be included in the call for the fourth and final quota of troops which
will complete the first draft and which are ordered to begin to entertain on February 23rd and to be completed within five days, Troops from 18 states will move to the cantonment on those dates. They will be as follows:

Camp Devens, (6575): New York, 772: Vermont 36; Rhode Island, 97; Connecticut, 1038: Massachusetts, 2082: New Hampshire, 29: and New York troops formerly allotted to Camp Dix, 2521.

Camp Upton (7500), New York troops formerly allotted to Camp Dix, 4287, other New York Troops, 5213: Camp Dix, (7000) all from New Jersey: Camp Meade, (6090), Pennsylvania, 4570, and West Virginia, 1520: Camp Lee, (3000), all from Pennsylvania: Camp Jackson, (3383), colored, all from South Carolina: Camp Gordon, (2800), colored, all from Georgia: Camp grand, (5000) all from Illinois: Camp Taylor, (6284), Illinois, 3352 and Kentucky, 2932.

Camp Dodge, (11,084), Iowa, 6384, Minnesota, 8600: Camp Funston, (2332), Kansas, 798 and Missouri 1624:

Camp Travis (7558), Oklahoma, 3380, and Texas, 4178: Camp Pike, (2000), colored, all from Arkansas.

Because many slackers from Arizona have been picked up in all parts of the country and forwarded to the camps, less than 100 men are needed at present to complete the full quota of the first draft for our state, and it is confidently expected by the official, at State draft headquarters that by February 23, the date set for the entertaining of the final quota in 18 states, that Arizona's quota will be complete.

Arizona is not alone in having her quota all or nearly all furnished, there being 29 other states in that fortunate class. This state probably will not be called upon for more men for the national army until the next draft if in fact it is even needed under the new classification.

When we got to the post office, we spoke with Art Chambers who was the postmaster. He was really the only government representative in the area. We inquired as to what we needed to do to register for the draft. He told us that as far as he knew the state had a small population and that he heard that our quota had been filled. He told us to go on back home and that if any problem came up that the forest service would let us know.

We obtained our mail, then went on to the Klondyke store to purchase our supplies then we went back home to help dad and Tom Sisson work at the mine. We dropped off the food supplies at the Garden Cabin, that Ola asked us to pick up for her. She told us she was suffering a lot of pain that day.

All total that year I think dad consulted seven different doctors to see what could be done about Ola's neck and back. She was just too young and vibrant to have to struggle with such pain the rest of her life.

On December 6th 1917 we stopped by the Garden Cabin on our way back from Jay Mahoney's place where we had been to buy beef jerky. We wanted to give some to Ola and just check on her well being. We found Ola lying crossways on her bed, writhing in pain and making strange noises. We held her up and asked her what was wrong. She just said, *"Poison."* That was all she said. We laid her back on the bed. I sent John to the Bosco's place, which is located about ten miles from the Garden Cabin at the mouth of Rattlesnake Canyon. He was to fetch Mrs. Bosco, who was the only person in the area with some medical background. When he got back sadly, Ola had already passed away. John went up to get dad and Tom at the mine to give them the bad news. When they came back to Ola's cabin, dad sent Tom Sisson to Safford to get a casket. When Tom was in Safford to get the casket he reported Ola's passing to Sheriff McBride.

Mrs. Bosco had prepared Ola's body for burial. The next day, we put Ola's body on her mattress and placed it in a blacktop hack, the kind used for carrying mail and passengers. We met Tom Sisson, who had brought the casket to Haby's ranch. Sheriff McBride was there along with twelve jurors and three doctors waiting for our arrival. They performed an inquest over Ola's body. After all of the testimony, the coroner's doctors rendered a verdict, *"Death from unknown poison."* One of the doctors took the body and surgically removed Ola's intestines and vital organs. He put them in a bed of ice and said he was going to send them to the state coroner's lab for a final determination of the exact cause of death. Ola May was buried in the small cemetery in Klondyke, next to our grandmother, Jane Power.

The following newspaper article was published in the Graham County Examiner on December 10th 1917 regarding the inquest performed over the body of Ola May Power;

Inquest Was Held

To Determine Cause of the Sudden Death of Klondyke Girl

The circumstances surrounding the sudden death of Miss Ola May Power, age 22 years, at the home of her father in Rattlesnake Canyon in the Gulairo Mountains, about 20 miles east of Klondyke, led to a trip by Sheriff McBride.

Doctor Platt and the County Coroner Joe Bleak, who also served as Justice of the Peace, early Friday morning, when the information was received by the sheriff of the girls' death.

They arrived at Klondyke at daylight Saturday morning and went to Haby's ranch, where the body of the girl had been brought from her home in Rattlesnake Canyon.

A coroner's inquest was led by the Coroner/Justice Joe Bleak and twelve jurors. At the inquest the girl's father testified that his wife died when Ola was a young child and that she lived with him all her life, at their home in Rattlesnake Canyon, in the Gulairo Mountains, where he had worked his mining claims.

About two months ago he took her to Safford, to Doctor Platt, to be treated by the doctor for throat trouble and again with her to Safford two weeks prior to her death again to get treatment on her throat. He also testified that Ola had suffered back and neck injuries since the buggy accident that killed his mother just three months earlier on September 17th 1917.

Late in the afternoon of last Thursday, the girl came to the house where he, his sons and their hired hand Tom Sisson and asked if one of them could bring her a bucket of water, which Tom did, and later they all went to her Garden Cabin for supper.

He said when they arrived at the cabin that evening, he said he went into her room and found her lying across the bed and suffering from a convulsion. He said he called for Sisson and sent him to Joe Bosco's ranch, ten miles away, to get assistance, and when Sisson left, he held the girl and tried to help her, but she died a short time later.

Mr. and Mrs. Bosco came to the house and prepared her body for burial. The body was taken to Haby's ranch for the inquest before burial. Sisson went onto Safford for a casket, leaving Safford Friday for Klondyke.

Word of the girl's sudden death was brought to Sheriff McBride, who left here with Dr. Platt and Joe Bleak, Graham County Coroner and Justice of the Peace, along with twelve jurors to attend the coroner's inquest. After hearing all the evidence in the case, the coroner's jury brought in a verdict that the girl had died from an unknown cause. The coroner removed her organs, and sent *them to the Pima County Coroner's office to be examined.*

By January of 1918 the road was finished from Mud Springs, located at the beginning of Rattlesnake Canyon past the Garden Cabin to the Mine Cabin which all totaled about 16 miles. We also finished building and installing the stamp mill. We were ready to start mining and processing the ore. All we were lacking was a boiler. We bought a boiler that was five feet in diameter and sixteen feet long. It took a team of eight horses and two days to transport the boiler to the mine. Once it arrived it took us three days to install it and get everything ready to start processing large volumes of ore. We were ready to start reaping the benefits from our mine after many years of backbreaking work, living in primitive conditions and selling off our cattle and livestock.

We bought the last quarter interest in the mine from Mr. Elwood in December of 1917 so now we owned the mine outright. Elwood had bought that quarter interest from the Talbot estate. Kane Wooten had tried to purchase the last quarter interest but Mr. Elwood, who had sold the other half interest to us wanted us to own the mine outright. There were hard feelings created with the Wooten family because Tom wanted to buy into the mine. There was a lot of talk that Tom was going to get his hands on the mine one way or another. Kane Wooten was a bit of a *"blow hard"* and nobody really took him serious. He and his brothers ran the cattle spread in adjacent Redfield Canyon. Tim had accepted the deputy sheriff job from Sheriff McBride that was originally offered to me. Since we didn't take Wooten's drinking and threats seriously, we were not concerned when we heard that he wanted to get his hands on our mine one way or the other.

Graham County in Eastern Arizona was rural by any standards. Mining and cattle were the prime industries and by these two endeavors most of the sparse population eked out a bare existence from the hard land. Women were old at forty, and the men were tough and worked hard or they didn't survive. Every man knew about horses and guns and most men wore one, except those who confined themselves to the towns. Almost every man carried a rifle in his saddle boot. Arizona had more water then, taller grass mainly because there were fewer people. Cattle were forty dollars a head, a good cigar was a nickel and a bottle of whiskey, in our dry Arizona, sold for twenty dollars a quart. Gold was eighteen dollars an ounce. The death penalty was abolished and a man was no longer hanged for stealing a horse. Politics was a big thing in Eastern Arizona. The Democratic Party was predominant and almost every lawman was in politics, or aspiring to be in politics.

Jeff Power was, by this time, in his middle fifties. He was rugged and strong, and according to his sons, a mild quiet man. John was 27 years old and Tom was 25. They were both tough and strong. They were proficient with pistols and rifles and were hard working men. John was short at five feet seven inches tall. He was stocky with blonde hair and blue eyes. He weighed 153 pounds. Tom had brown hair and brown eyes. He stood five feet nine inches tall and weighed 150 pounds. Tom Sisson was in his fifties and had dark brown hair with brown eyes. He stood five feet ten inches tall and weighed 170 pounds. Jeff Power owned a 30/30 caliber Winchester lever action saddle rifle. John owned a Winchester .404 caliber lever action rifle. Tom carried a 30/40 Craig lever action rifle and Tom Sisson owned a Savage .303 caliber bolt action rifle.

The mine cabin we lived in was made of split logs. It was notched at the corners and chinked with mud between the logs in the fashion of log cabins since the white man first came to the west. Our cabin had a plank wood floor. The roof was made of overlapping, and hand split, pine shingles. The fireplace was made of local rock and ran a few feet above the ridgepole.

The cabin had a door on the east side of the building which was our only door. It was made with a frame and the door was made of canvass nailed across the slats for insulation. There was a window on the east side of the building near the kitchen. It had glass panes and a wire screen. There was a similar window on the south wall between the fireplace and the east wall. The cabin was about twenty-five feet across the front and rear and the sides were about fifteen feet across. It consisted of two rooms. One room was a combination living and sleeping room. It had enough room for a bunk in each corner and just enough room to walk between.

The other room was the kitchen which had a wood burning stove, a small table and chairs along with cupboards with a few dishes, pots and pans. Attached to the north side of the house was a covered woodshed. Water was hauled from the spring and stream and kept in a large whiskey barrel. Lighting was provided by coal oil lamps.

We all started to get a little concerned when we heard that Kane Wooten went to Lee Solomon, who was a friend of his as well as a friend of ours, and asked Lee to help him bushwhack us and help steal our mine. Kane told Lee he was going to run for sheriff the next election and that if Lee helped him, that he would make him his deputy. Lee flat turned Kane down on both situations. Lee told Kane that we had spoken with the postmaster at Reddington, who told us that the forest service would come get us if we needed to register for the draft. Lee told Kane that if he had summons or warrants for our arrest, that he would come get us and bring us in to face the music. Lee told Kane;

*"Don't try to bring the Power boys
out or try to kill them because you will
not come back."*

Kane Wooten finally realized that Lee was not going to be part of any murder shenanigans. Kane showed Lee a letter Sheriff McBride had written to give to us. The letter outlined the seriousness of not registering for the draft. Lee agreed to deliver it to us. He reminded Kane that John and I had gone to the Redington post office where Art Chambers the postmaster told us not to worry about registering unless they heard from the forest service.

Chapter Seven

In early February 1918, Sheriff McBride received the official documentation from the Pima County Coroner concerning Ola's autopsy which clearly stated she did not die of food poisoning as the boys had said. The autopsy listed her cause of death was attributed to a broken neck. Tom said that he did remember that their father taking her to Doc Warner on several occasions because of the injury she received when she and grandma crashed the buggy. Tom went on to say that their father also took her to several other doctors, one in Tucson, one in Wilcox and several specialists in Globe. None of them were able to help Ola.

On February 7th Deputy Marshal Frank Haynes sent a message to Sheriff McBride. He asked the sheriff to give his letter to the district court judge and to obtain a warrant for the arrest of John and I for failing to register for the draft. Meanwhile Sheriff Frank McBride obtained a warrant to talk with dad and Tom Sisson, to clear up questions about the mysterious circumstances surrounding the death of Ola Mae, since we told the sheriff she told us she died from food poisoning and in reality the cause of death was a neck injury. Haynes also requested that Sheriff McBride to bring a man to serve as his deputyl.

US Deputy Marshal Frank Haynes never did anything in particular to prove his prowess as an officer of the law. He was a rather handsome man at age forty-four. He had been a heavy drinker and was well known to have had been bootlegging whiskey in the past.

Frank was born in Tennessee but brought up in West Texas where his family emigrated from Tennessee when Frank Haynes was five years old. He was a railroad brakeman in his early years. In

1900 he moved to Arizona, living in Bisbee and Globe and worked for the Eastern Arizona Railroad. He worked for the railroad until 1908 when he was appointed Deputy Sheriff of Gila County under then Sheriff Henry Thompson. When Thompson resigned due to health reasons, Haynes filled out the unexpired term. Later in 1910 he ran for the Sheriff of Gila County and won the election. He used his connections to be appointed Deputy US Marshal covering the eastern part of Arizona.

After Sheriff McBride obtained the warrants and appointed Mart Kempton, an experienced deputy sheriff as a Deputy Marshal to serve with Haynes. Then he sent a telegram to deputy Kane Wooten, who was living in Redfield Canyon requesting that he was to meet them at the Klondyke store on February 9th. From there they would all ride to the Power Mine Cabin to serve the warrants. When Kempton, Sheriff McBride and Deputy Marshall Haynes arrived at the Klondyke store they met our friend Lee Solomon. McBride explained to Lee that Marshal Haynes and Kane Wooten were there to serve warrants on Tom and John Power to answer for not registering for the draft.

Mart Kempton was a member of a prominent and highly respected family of the Gila Valley. He was a man of integrity and good judgment. Although a peace officer, and a good one, his primary interest lay in working his farm. He used his wages as a law officer to develop his forty acres located between Safford and Solomonville.

Kane Wooten was the middle brother of a large Mormon family. He was a natural-born peace officer, a man so large and husky that the very sight of him commanded respect and awe. Said to stand six feet four and weighing well over 200 pounds he was an imposing figure of a man. He was a polished cowboy and gun hand.

Lee Solomon told the Power Brothers later that when the officers arrived at the store, late in the morning, it appeared they had all been drinking. Lee told the sheriff;

"You had better not go up to the Power Cabin drinking, because nothing but trouble can come from being drunk or hung over."

He went on to tell them that if they needed liquid courage then the job they planned to do was not on the up and up. He warned some of them may not be coming back. Sheriff McBride told him they were not looking for any trouble and that he just wanted to talk with Jeff and Tom Sisson about Ola May's death. He explained that Deputy Marshall Haynes knew the circumstances regarding the family hardship running the mine and ranch along with the fact that the state quota had been filled that nothing would come of the boys failing to register for the draft, but that the government wanted them to know how serious it was to not register for the draft.

They decided to eat lunch, after which, Lee asked the sheriff if he could ride along with them because his ranch was located in Rattlesnake Canyon just a few miles from the Power Garden Cabin. Lee Solomon told the sheriff that if he was there that the Power boys would not cause any trouble but warned them;

"If you four go up there drinking and trying to throw your weight around there will be trouble and the Power family would be more than obliged to finish any job you boys start."

Sheriff McBride told Lee that he knew the Power family well, especially since Tom Power worked under his guidance bootlegging whiskey, headed his election campaign and that he offered Tom the job to be his deputy.

Sheriff McBride said he had questions that needed to be answered regarding the mysterious death of Ola May. He went on to tell Lee that he simply wanted to get the facts clear about Ola's death. He went on to tell Lee he did not expect any trouble that they would not go up until the next morning and they would all be sober. Lee reminded him that there had been talk around Safford and Klondyke that Kane Wooten and Mart Kempton planned to kill the Power family and steal their mine. McBride told Lee that he heard the talk as well but if he was there any bloodshed would be avoided. He said he was the most experienced lawman going and that he knew he would be able to talk with the Power family and there would be no problems. He went on to say he respected the family and did not want any trouble. He told Lee he was very disappointed that the boys did not come in and register. Lee informed the sheriff he did not think that Tom and John ever saw the letter and would be completely surprised by our visit.

Before they left the Klondyke store, Lee overheard Sheriff McBride talking to the men explaining his plan was to stop at Joe Bosco's place, about five miles from the Power Mine Cabin to spend the night. Mart Kempton said Joe Bosco wanted to have a poker game and all we needed to bring was our money and lots of booze. Since Lee's ranch was just down the road from the Power Garden Cabin and near the Bosco place he asked the sheriff if they minded if he rode along and join in the game if they had room for one more player. Lee told us that T.K. said;

> "The more the merrier, just make sure you bring your money."

Lee's real reason for going was to make sure the officers did not go to serve their warrants under the influence of alcohol. Lee went on to tell us that the officers rode in a car and he followed them on his horse. He said they arrived at the Bosco ranch a little before dark on the evening of February the 9th. Mrs. Bosco made dinner for everyone. They started the poker game about an hour after dinner. Lee said they smoked cigars, drank booze and played poker until three in the morning. He said they were all drunk from drinking whiskey and gambling all night. Mrs. Bosco cooked breakfast for them and gave them all lots of coffee to help them sober up before they left to serve the warrants. It was the morning of February 10th and none of the officers had slept the night before.

Later, after the incident, Mrs. Bosco testified at the trial that she fed the officers and kept them at their ranch giving them lots of coffee to help sober them up. She said they were definitely hung over when they left that morning but she said their stomachs were full and they drank coffee for at least an hour before the left. She said Lee Solomon left with officers and that Lee did not drink near as much as her husband and the others.

Haynes testified that Kane Wooten loaned him his 30/30 Winchester lever action rifle. Then Wooten borrowed Joe Bosco's forty-four carbine, a short saddle rifle. Joe told Wooten that it had a hair trigger and that he needed to be very careful when he carried that weapon. He said even though he had owned the gun for many years and was familiar with it, there were times that it went off way too quickly. Kane thanked Joe for the information and said he would take caution when handling the rifle. Sheriff McBride carried a thirty-forty Craig lever action rifle and Kempton had a forty-five seventy caliber carbine that had a piece leather wrapped around the butt of the rifle. All four men carried .45 caliber Colt revolvers.

Joe Bosco told them they had to travel through a narrow passage in Squaw Canyon just before they reached the Power Mine Cabin. Haynes laughed and said;

*"All I ask is for you to not let Sheriff
McBride run off with the car."*

They all went out to Bosco's Corral to borrow horses for the ride to the Power Mine Cabin. Joe said Deputy Kempton selected a brown horse, an animal belonging to his boy Jim. Though a tough, good animal, the horse had a tendency toward a bad disposition from time to time. He knew that Kempton was a good horseman and could handle the horse. Marshal Haynes selected a horse from the A-1 stock. It was a good steady horse called Grey. Kane Wooten rode a small sorrel mule and Sheriff McBride rode a sorrel horse. Joe said he and his wife had an uneasy feeling when the officers departed that morning.

Lee Solomon testified that when they got to his place the officers insisted that he stay behind. Sheriff McBride told him that Kane Wooten knew the trail and that he could lead them from there to the Mine Cabin. He said they had plenty of officers to fulfill their duty. The officers thanked Lee for his hospitality.

Deputy Marshal Haynes further testified in court that after they left Lee Solomon's ranch they headed up the Squaw Creek Trail when they first came to the Power's Garden Cabin. He said after a careful inspection they realized that nobody was home. They went inside and built a fire in the fireplace to warm the cabin. They needed to rest as their lack of sleep was catching up to them. It had snowed all that night leaving some three inches of snow on the ground the next morning. The Marshal was not sure of the exact time but he thought they left between four and four-thirty that morning. Kane Wooten, their guide, figured it would take until daylight because of the snow to reach the Mine Cabin.

They rode about three miles up the trail when Kane Wooten stopped and told them he thought they were very close to the cabin. He because it was very dark in the canyon, but the moon shone brightly with the sky full of stars. Wooten thought the Cabin was just down the hill on the trail just ahead, but was not too sure as he had not been there for some five years. Sheriff McBride remarked it would be better to get there a little later rather than too early. They dismounted, drank some water and discussed their strategy for about forty-five minutes.

Sheriff McBride told them he did not want any trouble and that he would be able to coax the men out of the cabin so they could talk. Kempton and Wooten took off on foot down the trail toward the cabin to find a place near the front of the cabin. McBride and Marshal Haynes were planning on coming up on each side of the cabin, that way all exits would be covered. As he neared the cabin the sheriff could see a man moving about due to the light from the fire place. The shadow happened to be that of Jeff Power; he had started the fire just before dawn to make breakfast.

Haynes later testified things started to go wrong as they approached the cabin. They had spooked a horse that took off running past them in front of the cabin. It had a bell around its neck that started ringing. Mart Kempton and Kane Wooten were partially hidden behind some rocks near the stream in front of the cabin. Marshall Haynes testified that he and Sheriff McBride came up the trail from the back of the cabin. Haynes approached from the right side of the cabin to the front corner and the sheriff went up the left side to the opposite corner. Except for the spooked horse all went to plan to surround the cabin.

Just before dawn on Sunday, February 10th 1918, it was biting cold in the remote high country of the Galiuro Mountains of Eastern Arizona. There was a snow on the peaks of the mountains surrounding the Power cabin. A light snow had fallen during the night and there was about two inches covering the ground at daybreak.

Just like every other day of the year, Jeff Power, who seemed to have an alarm clock in his head, woke up before daylight. He was still in his long johns and began making a fire in the fireplace. John got up a few minutes later and lit an oil lamp so he could build a fire in the kitchen wood burning stove. Sisson and Tom were still in their bunks waiting for the cabin to warm up.

Jeff was reaching for his trousers when he heard sounds that were out of place in the pre-dawn darkness. Two of John's mares that were allowed to graze free around the cabin had the bells around their necks ringing loudly as galloped past the cabin. Then the dogs began to bark. Thinking that a mountain lion might be after them, Jeff picked up his 30/30 Winchester and went to the front door. As he stood in the doorway looking right and left into the darkness he couldn't see anything. With all the commotion Sisson and Tom jumped up to help their father. John slammed the stove door shut and stood up quickly.

As Tom Power got to the front door and just as he arrived, he heard a voice from outside the cabin yell, three times in a row;

"Throw up your Hands!"

Startled, and knowing he was target standing in the lighted doorway, Jeff Power dropped his rifle and started to raise his hands. Before he got his hands all the way up, three quick shots rang out. He spun around falling on his back in the dirt just outside the cabin door.

John ran to the door, saw their father on the ground and started to step outside to help him. Four more shots were fired. Quickly he ducked back inside, ran to his bed, and got his rifle. He ran to the side of the door and fired two shots to the north where some shots came from. Next, he spun quickly around and pumped two more shots toward the south. Just as John was firing, four more shots hit the doorjamb and an old saddle hanging by the door. Wood splinters hit John's left eye along with pieces of leather from the saddle. One of the slugs blew off a part of the bridge of his nose.

According to Tom Power, by this time he was on his feet with his rifle. As he crossed in front of the east window, a slug tore through the screen and shattering the glass, throwing broken into his left eye and left side of his face. The bullet passed within inches of his neck and buried itself in the far wall of the cabin. Tom said;

"The shock of the glass hitting my eye and face stopped me for an instant. He testified that he couldn't see anything out of his left eye and his right eye began watering from the pain."

He wiped his eyes with his arm, turned and ran as he approached the window it was also shattered by a slug from outside. Tom glimpsed the silhouette of a figure outside and fired one shot. It appeared the man went down and did not move.

Tom and John Power swore that Tom Sisson took no part in the fight. However, later evidence of three empty 303 caliber rounds found next to his bed implicated him in the gunfight. It appeared Tom Sisson had managed to get his rifle loaded and stuck it in a crack between the logs just about knee high. He said he was able to see a man's silhouette and shot once hitting the man in the leg. It was all he could see from his vantage point but he got off two more shots. He saw the man go down and not get up. After the shooting stopped, Tom turned around to see

John standing up against the front doorjamb; his face was covered with blood.

It was unearthly still as the echoes of the last shots died away. Tom said they waited for several minutes, knowing their father had been shot down, and feared the worst. They went to the door and peered out cautiously. It was eerily silent. They could see their father's body lying a few feet in front of the cabin. Tom said they could see in the dimly lit early morning two other bodies lying around the cabin. Due to their eye injuries, they were not able to make out the identity of the two men lying outside the cabin. After a few minutes when it was fairly apparent their attackers were not moving, they decided it was safe to check the welfare of their father. He was still alive when they reached him.

They picked him up, carried him back into the cabin and put him on his bunk. He had been shot in his left lung. They could see his wound was very serious, but he was still conscious. He kept saying over and over;

> *"Why did Kane Wooten shoot me when I had my hands up after my gun was placed behind me next to the door jam."*

Tom went on to say that Jeff their father didn't want to stay in the cabin, for some reason. He got up and walked out the door toward the mine. He got halfway there, before he collapsed saying;

> *"This is as far as I can go."*

The boys testified that they ran back to the cabin, got some blankets and bedding. They made a stretcher, put their dad on it and took him inside the mine. Their father was obviously dying. After they saw to it that he was comfortable, leaving Tom Sisson with him, they walked around the property to inspect the dead bodies of the men who attacked them. The first two we saw were the bodies of Kane Wooten and Sheriff McBride. Tom said;

> *"We couldn't believe our eyes. We had campaigned for Sheriff McBride; we thought him to be a good friend. We were totally shocked as we gazed upon his body lying on the ground."*

They had problems in the past with Kane Wooten and his brothers but they were surprised that he had gone so far as to shoot our father when he was unarmed. They never dreamed that those two would be involved in such a dastardly deed. Tom went on to testify that they didn't recognize the other dead man. Prior to the shooting, Tom said he heard a voice coming from one side of their cabin saying;

> *"Boys, Boys, Boys."*

The only surviving Law Officer, Deputy Marshall Haynes testified that the statement came from Sheriff McBride, just as he got to the corner of the cabin and saw Kane Wooten with his rifle pointed at old man Power.

Sheriff McBride prided himself, and his record showed that he was at his best when he was negotiating to avoid a fight. He definitely did not want a confrontation. He simply wanted to talk with the family to ascertain any information he could about the death of Ola May Power, because the autopsy proved she did not die of food poisoning. As far as he was concerned the fact that the boys had not registered for the draft was not a real concern for him. It was a warrant that Marshall Haynes was there to serve. But it was too late for talk at this point.

Deputy Marshal Haynes testified in court that he saw Jeff Power standing about five feet outside the cabin door when he reached the front side of the cabin. He said he could also see Sheriff McBride on the other side of the building. By this time Tom Power said he, his brother and Tom Sisson were out of their bedrolls and dressed. Haynes said the moment he heard a gun go off and saw Old Man Power spin around and fall on the ground about three feet from the door. Then more shots were fired from the cabin.

According to Haynes testimony, the next shots also came from the cabin. Kane Wooten and the other man, who we did not recognize, and later found out was a deputy named, Mart Kempton, were both standing in front of the cabin between the fallen Jeff Power and the stream. They both stood up when guns were fired and they were both hit from shots coming from the cabin door. In the mean while both Sheriff McBride and I cut loose with our pistols toward the cabin door. I saw McBride get shot in the leg. This was consistent with the fact that a gun had been placed between the logs in an opening close to the ground. As Sheriff McBride fell another bullet hit him in the upper body and a final bullet hit him in the head.

At this point Sheriff McBride, deputies Kempton and Wooten were all lying dead on the ground. Haynes further testified that he looked in the cabin and saw nobody moving. This was obviously not factual because if he had looked in the cabin he would have been shot by Tom or John Power or Tom Sisson, who were all, in fact, very much alive. He saw the sheriff and both deputies had been shot. Later he testified he left to get help for the downed officers. He said as he backed up and ran back up the trail to where the horses were tied. As he was leaving the gunfight, he saw a figure come outside the cabin door and drag Jeff Power back into the cabin. Tom Power, John Power and Tom Sisson all testified that Jeff Power kept saying over and over;

> *"Why did Kane Wooten shoot me when I had my hands in the air?"*

The answer was very simple. Kane Wooten went into battle with an untested weapon. The gun he borrowed had a hair- trigger. All of the officers were there without sleep from the night before. They were all tired, full of coffee and just a flinch of his finger on the trigger was all that was necessary for a gun with a hair trigger to go off. There is no way that I can believe that Deputy Wooten intended to kill Jeff Power. Even though he had talked about doing in the Power family he was again known to say things when drinking that he never meant.

In any event, the officers got into a gun fight far more dangerous than they were expecting. Three of the four officers lay dead. Jeff Power was mortally wounded. It was just a matter of time before he would die because he was so far from medical help. Any help sent would arrive too late to save any lives. Unfortunately, the only witnesses to give an account of the gunfight were Tom and John Power, Tom Sisson and Deputy Marshall Frank Haynes.

Haynes testified at the trial that he rode to the Bosco Ranch after leaving Rattlesnake Canyon. He asked Mr. Bosco to ride to the Power Mine Cabin and see if there was anything that could be done for the three fallen officers and Jeff Power. He told Bosco there was a gunfight and his three companions were either dead or dying along with Jeff Power. He told Mr. Bosco he was heading back to Klondyke to report the shooting and to get medical help and reinforcements.

Not known for experience as a lawman and really a political appointee for the job a Deputy US Marshal, he knew he was in big trouble. It was his warrants and insistence to take the now three dead officers to the Power cabin. He was well aware that he was not good with a gun. He knew beyond a doubt that he would not have been able to subdue the men in the cabin by himself. With no idea how many men were left in the cabin, Haynes figured he better ride to Klondyke and get help for the fallen officers.

Chapter Eight

Tom Power picks up the story again. We stayed with our father, in the mine shaft, until he died sometime around two o'clock Sunday afternoon. There was no time to get medical help for him so we made him as comfortable as possible. We covered our father's body with a blanket. We covered the officer's bodies with additional blankets and tarps leaving them where they lay.

We rode to our neighbor Jay Mahoney's place to seek his help and ask him to stay with the dead bodies of our father and the fallen officers until official help came. We knew the general reaction would not be good, when it was learned that we had shot Sheriff McBride, his deputy Kane Wooten, and the unknown man. We knew we would not get fair treatment from any posse of local Graham County officers. We feared a lynch mob would be hot on our heels when the news hit Safford, so we decided to ride to Tucson and turn ourselves in to Sheriff Rye Miles. We had known him for a long time and he was a good friend of our father. We figured we would at least get fair treatment from him.

There was a very good chance we might have to defend ourselves on the way to Tucson. We took Sheriff McBride's rifle, and his .45 caliber Colt revolver. Kane Wooten had a 9mm Luger and a rifle we picked up; we noted the rifle had a hair-trigger and left it. The third man's Colt 45 pistol had been in his coat pocket and it fell out when he hit the ground; we took it as well. I unbuckled McBride's gun belt and took it and his Colt. John and I took any money we found figuring the dead men would not need it and we would use it to get to Tucson. We took two horses, a sorrel mule, 600 rounds of ammunition along with our heavy coats and several canteens.

When we reached Jay Mahoney's place that afternoon, Jay, Henry Allen a hired hand, Sol Ray and Ed Knothe were there. Jay asked us what all the commotion was earlier that morning. He said he thought they heard some gunfire around daybreak. I told Jay that the evidence of the shootout was laying in our front yard and that Sheriff McBride, T.K. Wooten and a man who was unknown to us were dead in front of our cabin. I told Jay he would find dad's body in the mineshaft. I asked him to watch over the bodies of the three dead officers until help arrived. We only stayed a short time and I only spoke to Mahoney. We did not say where we were going. We liked Jay Mahoney and had some past run-ins with him, but he was known to stretch the truth, brag, or downright lie if caught a wrongdoing. We gave Jay no details about the gun fight; we didn't believe he would tell the truth.

We confided in Henry Allen and asked him to ride to Klondyke and report the shooting. However, we were unaware Deputy Marshall Haynes had taken part in the shootout, was already in Klondyke, and had telegraphed the authorities in Safford. Haynes had formed a posse to come after us. He was waiting for reinforcements to bring in the bodies of the dead officers.

When the posse got to the Mahoney's Jay told them we had rifles and he saw us armed with pistols. However, it would have been impossible for him to see we had pistols because John and I had overcoats on that covered our pistols. Jay Mahoney told many lies regarding the shootout. He spoke like he was a witness, but he was nowhere near when the gunfight took place.

Prior to this, Jay Mahoney and his father spent the most eerie night of their lives. They took turns staying awake to guard the bodies of the dead officers and Jeff Power. The next morning Jay heard a noise on the trail, and said to his father;

> *"Somebody's coming down the trail.*
> *Hopefully it's the posse and not the*
> *Power brothers returning."*

Excited now, weary of the inaction and tired from the long night watching over the bodies Jay strode up the trail, anxious to meet the source of the welcome sounds. On rounding a bend in the trail he found himself suddenly facing a group of men, tense, with nerves frayed by reports of the killings. They having ridden many hours through the night, suffered from hunger and lack of sleep.

Riding two abreast, four of the eight of them threw down on Jay. Staring into hostile gun barrels was not a reassuring feeling for Jay. Al Kuntz, a neighbor and miner, probably saved his life early that morning when he shouted as he laid his gun across his leg;

> *"Don't shoot! It's Mahoney!"*

Jay Mahoney had always admired Kuntz, but at that moment found himself with a much deeper affection for the man. Al Kuntz had moved to Rattlesnake Canyon, but had previously served in the army as a master mule packer when stationed in the Philippines.

Not until they arrived on the scene did they learn the identity of Mart Kempton. Al introduced Jay to two of the posse men, Howard McBride and Nate Kempton, brothers of two of the dead officers. Jay was asked many questions, but he said the first one was the most difficult. Howard asked;

> *"Is Frank dead?"*

Jay said he could only nod and swallow the big lump in his throat. As they made their way slowly to the cabin, he learned that the posse was comprised of eighteen men in all. They had split into three groups at the top of the divide, attempting to flank the Power brothers and Tom Sisson if they still were in or around the cabin. One group kept to the ridge west of the cabin. One group which Jay encountered on the trail leading to the cabin and the third group following about a quarter mile behind them in case they encountered the outlaws coming up from behind.

As the group approached the bodies, Jay told his first lie explaining why he had taken the liberty of covering them, assuring the members of the posse that he had made no move to disturb the slain officers. A dramatic, sorrowful scene ensued. Howard McBride and Nate Kempton gazed at the exposed portions of their brothers' bodies then they ripped the blankets and tarps from their brothers' bodies. Howard threw himself across his brother's body sobbing in great gasps. Nate Kempton seeing his brother's dead body held back his weeping but with his lips compressed and his face white as a sheet, it was obvious by his body language, and the clasping of his hands that he was devastated.

The men comprising the posse had swung into action fast at the news of the tragedy, with the possibility that the officers might only be wounded and not dead. But if the officers were dead, it was their duty to bring the bodies back to Safford for an inquest.

Confronted with the dead officers, it was logical for the posse to conduct an inquest, even though it would not be official because Joe Bleak, the county coroner, had left after them. Nate Kempton and Howard McBride wanted to get their brothers back to their families. However, they knew the importance of recording the positions of the bodies, wounds inflicted, and other pertinent facts to help with the official inquest.

According to Jay Mahoney, Joe Phillips, Safford's depot agent was selected to head the inquest and choose members for an unofficial jury. Their report indicated the thoroughness they took in completing the inquest when they returned to Safford. In his report Joe Phillips stated;

> "The officers' cartridge belts and guns were all missing, and there was evidence that they had all been searched, undoubtedly by the outlaws. Their belts were unbuckled and the front fly of their trousers was unbuttoned, which provided easy access to their pockets. With the exception of a few lose coins, no money was found on the officers then after searching the fallen officers, they proceeded to examine the wounds of the men, noting the exact position of the bullet holes in each body including the number of wounds and the position of each body in relation to the cabin. They also noted the blood and other marks, possible five to eight feet from the main door of the cabin, indicating that a body had fallen and was then removed."

The officers claimed they noted a bullet hole in the ground under Sheriff McBride's head, leading them to believe that the Sheriff had been shot in the head while he was lying on the ground. If in fact if there had been a hole in the ground, an experienced lawman would have dug into the ground to recover the bullet, that way they would be able to ascertain which gunman fired the three shots that killed Sheriff McBride. Old man Mahoney and his son guarded the bodies all night long to preserve the evidence. By moving the bodies before Joe Bleak arrived the lawmen destroyed all the evidence. One has to wonder if the unofficial inquest was intentionally botched.   Some other inconsistencies can be found in Joe Phillips comments in court;

"After we wrapped and packed the bodies and loaded them onto the pack horses, we went to the cabin and we made a note of the bullet scars around the door and casing."

He went on to say;

"We also noted the bullet scars in the wall across the room from the door. Empty shell casings were found scattered over the floor of the two rooms in the cabin."

Phillips said;

"We noted the caliber and number of each of the shells found on the floor in each room."

He also testified that he did not remember the calibers or numbers of the shells found;

"But we left all the shells where they lay, undisturbed, so that a full inspection by proper authorities could be made at a later date."

He explained they were puzzled at first finding three empty casings under a small table in the northeast corner of the kitchen. But, after one of the men crawled under the table, the reason became very clear. A crack or space, about an inch wide between the second and third logs right next to the corner gave the reason.

"A one-foot section of mud chinking had fallen out. It appeared one of the outlaws had crouched there where he could easily see the legs of anyone standing at that end of the cabin. We determined from the position of Sheriff

> *McBride's body, the three shells that penetrated his body were fired from that exact spot in the cabin."*

Joe Phillips further testified, upon completion of the examination of the bodies, he led the jury (posse) to the mine tunnel. They needed to determine the disposition of Jeff Power's body.

Jay Mahoney told them where Power was shot and how he died. He said he promised the boys he would bury their father;

> *"We gave Jay permission to bury the body."*

Mahoney asked about taking the body to Klondyke. Joe asked Jay;

> *"Why?"*

Jay said;

> *"I want to bury him with Ola and Granny Power. Joe told him they did not have a pack horse to spare. Mahoney told Joe he could get one but Joe told him that the County Attorney would want to see the bullet holes in his body, and not to bury him."*

Jay then asked Joe;

> *"What should I do with his body?"*

One of the posse men said;

> *"Hang the old son-of-a-bitch by his heels in a mesquite tree and let the coyotes have him."*

This statement was the shared thought of a majority of the men in the posse. It was understandable since three well respected officers had been killed. Although the statement made regarding

Jeff Power's body by one of the posse men was very inappropriate.

An official inquest was never performed on Jeff Power's body, nor was there an official inquest of the officer's bodies, at the scene. One of the first and foremost rules of law enforcement is to not desecrate the scene of a crime by moving the bodies until the coroner and the proper authorities could exam at all the evidence.

Once the bodies were removed the evidence was gone and there was no way to get an accurate version of what actually happened that early Sunday morning in February.

That act of destroying the evidence and having never performed an autopsy on Jeff Power was quite suspicious. In addition, the records of the trial disappeared as did the official inquest of Ola May Power's death. Given the strange disappearance of evidence, transcripts, and official records, one has to wonder if they were trying to hide something.

One also wonders about the posse's motives. Jay Mahoney testified that before leaving the crime scene he witnessed some posse members *"pillaging"* the cabin of a good portion of its contents. One man took John's guitar. Another man took Ola's violin, while others helped themselves to items ranging from a sheepskin pack saddle to razors and clocks.

One of the posse members not satisfied with the amount of his immediate loot, upon arriving home, took the Model T Ford the Power's had stored in a garage in Wilcox. However, later he was forced to return it to the custody of the Graham County Court. It was auctioned from the steps of the courthouse along with several other Power family items and the money derived from the auction was given to each of the officers' widows.

As the men prepared to leave the crime scene that afternoon, Joe Phillips testified a few of the posse members decided to stay at the cabin, believing the Power boys and Sisson might return. This possibility was mentioned by the outlaws to Jay Mahoney as they left his place, probably because they didn't trust Jay.

Joe Phillips also testified a few officers helped him, Jay Mahoney, and Al Upshaw, wrap the bodies of the three dead officers in quilts and blankets. They then placed them on pack horses face down and tied their arms and feet under the horses' stomachs so the bodies would not fall off the pack horses. They transported the bodies out of the canyon to Klondyke where trucks hauled them to Safford for the inquest, funeral and burial service.

Upshaw explained a strange tendency of pack horses. He said the horses can have a weird reaction to bodies being carried on their backs. Sometimes they simply will lie down and roll over trying to get the bodies off their backs. Al told them although he had been a cowboy all his life there was no clear explanation why they did this. However, they would have to keep a sharp eye on the pack animals to prevent this from happening.

Joe Black, the Graham County Coroner was notified by Marshal Haynes to come to Klondyke as soon as possible. He was needed to perform an official inquest at the Mine Cabin on the bodies of the fallen officers. Joe arrived in Klondyke the next day and headed right on up to the crime scene to perform the inquest. He met the posse about fourteen miles from the cabin. They had the bodies of the fallen officers with them. It appeared that for whatever reason Haynes did not want an inquest performed at the Mine Cabin.

The story of the killing of three officers and the death of Jeff Power plus the pursuit of the outlaws became a state and national event. Information about the murders of the three officers was carried by every newspaper in Arizona and all papers nationally. This story had more national coverage than the capture of Geronimo in 1886 and the flight and death of the notorious Arizona outlaw *"The Apache Kid."* A newspaper article from the Graham Guardian on February 13th 1918 concerning the shooting follows:

OFFICERS KILLED IN GUN BATTLE WITH SLACKERS

Sheriff McBride and Deputies Kempton and Wooten Slain by John and Tom Power along with Tom Sisson, at the Power' Home in the Galiuro Mountains, Sunday Morning-Deputy Marshal Frank Haynes, Member of Party, Brings in News of the Killing

The entire community was shocked at the news received here Sunday afternoon that Sheriff McBride, Chief Deputy Martin R. Kempton and Deputy Kane Wooten had been killed in a gun battle with the Power boys, John, aged 28 years; Thomas, aged 25 years, and a paroled horse thief, Thomas Sisson, aged 55 years, which occurred at the home of Jeff G. Power, father of the two boys, near the old Bowman gold mine, in the Galiuro Mountains, 28 miles southeast of Klondyke, shortly before 7:00 o'clock Sunday morning.

The first news of the killing was brought in here by Deputy U.S. Marshal Frank Haynes, of Globe, who was the fourth member of the party which left here Saturday afternoon for the Power home to bring back John and Tom Power, who were wanted by the government on the charge of evading the selective draft.

According to the story told by Deputy Marshal Haynes when he arrived at the court house, he had come here from Globe on orders from U.S. Marshall Dillon to get the two slackers, John and Tom Power. He secured the services of Kane Wooten, a deputy sheriff to accompany him, along with Sheriff McBride and his Chief Deputy Kempton offered their services, the government to pay the expenses of the trip. Sheriff McBride wanted Old Man Power and Tom Sisson for the purpose of clearing up the mystery of Ola Power's death, aged 22 years, who died early in December under suspicious circumstances.

The four officers left here Saturday afternoon, about 3:00 o'clock, in Sheriff McBride's car for Klondyke. They arrived at the Upchurch's place, Klondyke, sometime after 6:00 o'clock p.m., where they secured three horses and a mule. They left Upchurch's place after 7:00 o'clock, taking the trail for the home of Jeff Power in the Galiuro Mountains. On their way they stopped at Joe Bosco's house, a cattleman, but found no one at home. Next they came to the first house and then the second house, both of which belonged to old man Power. One of the houses had been occupied by Power's daughter, Ola, who died there last December.

The Party continued on until, just about 7:00 Sunday morning, they arrived in the vicinity of the Power home, a log house. This house was built about 10 feet west of a creek, up on the embankment. It fronted the east. The officers tied up their horses in a small canyon northwest of the house and then started for the house. Sheriff McBride stationed himself at the northeast corner of the house, Deputy Haynes going to the northwest corner of the house. At the northeast corner, about two feet from the house, was the remains of a fence, built of shakes, about five feet long. Sheriff McBride was between this fence and the house.

Deputies Kempton and Wooten evidently went around the western side of the house, the house on this side being close to a high hill, over which was a trail leading into the new trail which met the new road going into Klondyke. The trail on this hill was higher than the house. The two officers stationed themselves at the southeast corner of the house. On the east front of the house is the front door. On the southeast side a fireplace has been build and east of the fireplace is a window. There is a window on the northeast side, but no door.

Haynes went on to report that at the time Deputies Kempton and Wooten had reached their stations, old man Power came out of the door nearest to them. Evidently, the men in the house had heard the officers when they went around the west side of the house, for when old man Power came out of the door, he was carrying a gun. As he stepped out in the open the officers called to him to throw up his hands. Placing his gun between his knees, he raised his hands and as he did this, the door, behind him opened wide *enough for a gun to be shoved through.*

Something occupied right then, either old man Power dropped his hands to seize his gun or the man behind the door began shooting, for the battle commenced. The man in the door, with the gun just far enough out to be turned, was firing in the direction where Kempton was stationed, and then turned the gun and fired at the place where Sheriff McBride was posted. Sheriff McBride told Deputy Marshal Haynes to watch the window, and he went in close to the house to do so, when he noticed that the sheriff had fallen and his feet protruded past the fence. Some twenty-five shots were fired, then the shooting stopped and everything was quiet.

Haynes went on to say that he went up to the window to look in, but he could see nothing. There was no noise in the house, everything was perfectly quiet. He then went to the place northwest of the house, where the horses were tied, got his horse and rode up the trail on the hill west of the house, stopped for several minutes but could see no one near the house, then saw a man east of the house lying on the ground, and thought it was Wooten, but on second glance saw it was not Wooten and might be old man Power. He heard no noise and believed the men in the house were dead. He did not see Kempton or Wooten and did not know whether they had been killed or wounded. Seeing nobody moving, Deputy Marshal Haynes then started for Klondyke to get help. He reached Klondyke about 10:30 o'clock and told of the killing of Sheriff McBride and the people started to organize a posse to go to the Power house.

Deputy Haynes then started for Safford, arriving at the court house about 4:00 o'clock pm and told of the battle at Power's home and the killing of Sheriff McBride. Sometime after Deputy Haynes left the scene of the battle, John and Tom Power and Tom Sisson came out of the house and carried old man Power across the creek to within 25 yards of the tunnel to the mine. Then they came back to the house and took the guns and ammunition of the dead officers. Then they went to the place where the officers' horses and the mule where tied and got the two horses and the mule.

They then rode over to the Mahoney's house, about a mile from the Power home, where they summoned the Mahoney's father and son, and a young man named Henry Allen, who had been working for the Mahoney's building a fence at Hot Springs. They told them that they had killed three officers and had taken their horses and a mule, their guns and ammunition. They said they got all three officers and evidently did not know there were four officers in the party that came to their home to get them. They had not seen Deputy Marshal Haynes.

They also told of the killing of Deputy Wooten, by John Power, who shot him through the window on the south side of the house, after Wooten had fired at him through the window, the broken glass cutting his eye. Tom Power said he shot Sheriff McBride and Tom Sisson had shot Deputy Kempton. They told the Mahoney's their father had been killed and asked them to go over and take care of his body. Then they rode away. The Mahoney's and Allen went over the Power house, reaching there about 10:30 o'clock and found Power lying about 50 yards east of the house, across the creek. He was unconscious. They carried him in to the mine and placed him on a cot.

Allen then reported that he went over to the house and found the body of Sheriff McBride lying near the northeast corner of the house, and then found the bodies of Deputies Kempton and Wooten lying at the southeast corner of the house. Allen said the rode to Klondyke and told the people there that Sheriff McBride and Deputies Kempton and Wooten had been killed by the Power boys and Tom Sisson and that the murderers had left the place on the officer's horses, Sisson riding the mule, and had gone in the direction of Redington on the San Pedro river.

Allen then rode on into Safford, reaching here shortly after 4:00 o'clock pm and coming to the courthouse, told the story of finding the bodies of the three officers. Deputy Marshal Haynes was in the sheriff's office, surrounded by a crowd of men, to whom he was giving a description of the battle, when Allen arrived, and the deputy marshal then learned for the first time that Deputies Kempton and Wooten had been killed.

At Klondyke, a posse was organized consisting of local citizens. This posse was to go after the bodies of the dead officers and bring them into Safford. The posse left Klondyke at 5:00 o'clock pm and reached the Power home about 7:00 Monday morning. They learned the Mahoney's and a man named Edward Knothe that Jeff Power the father of the Power boys, had died about 4:00 Sunday afternoon. The bodies of the dead officers were found and preparations were made to bring them into Klondyke, which were completed in several hours. The posse then started back for Klondyke, arriving there about 7:00 o'clock pm.

At Klondyke, the posse was met by Doctor Platt, W.V. Thorpe and other from Safford, and the bodies were transferred to card and brought here about 11:30 o'clock Monday night, and placed in the justice of the peace's room, in the basement of the courthouse, where an examination of the wounds was made by Drs. Platt, Schenck and Stratton. Sheriff McBride had been shot four times, once through the right leg, another the lower part of the body, the third the upper part of the body and last through the neck.

Deputy Kempton had been shot through the neck, the bullet severing the spinal cord. Deputy Wooten had been shot through the back, the bullet fracturing the spinal column. The wounds were all made by a large caliber soft nose bullet. An inquest was held at the courthouse Tuesday afternoon and the jury brought in a verdict that Sheriff R. F. McBride, Chief

Deputy Sheriff Martin R. Kempton and Deputy Sheriff T.K. "Kane" Wooten, had died from gunshot wounds inflicted at the hands of John Power, Tom Power and Tom Sisson.

Sheriff R. F. Bride was 42 years of age. He leaves a widow and seven children. Chief Deputy Sheriff Martin R. Kempton was 40 years of age and also leaves a widow and seven children. Deputy Sheriff Kane Wooten was 36 years of age, and he leaves a widow and four children.

Chapter Nine

When Deputy Marshal Haynes reached Klondyke the morning of the shootout and notified the authorities in Safford of the tragic news about the gunfight, he set in motion the most extensive manhunt in Arizona's eventful history. Posses large and small, totaling over 3000 men, formed almost spontaneously to take part in the far-flung hunt. Colonel Morgan of the United States Army stationed at Fort Huachuca set a pattern of the military by dispatching two troops of cavalrymen for patrol duty along the border between the United States and Old Mexico. Army commanders from Fort Bliss, Texas and Hachita, New Mexico were also dispatched to guard the border and to also keep an eye open for signs of the outlaws. They were informed that the outlaws were probably on their way to take refuge in Old Mexico. It helped that the border between the United States and Mexico was closed due to World War One.

Below is an article published in the Graham Guardian on Thursday February 15th 1918

Soldiers Guarding the Border

Latest Report States Posses Are Hot On the Trail of Outlaws South of Busenback's Ranch

As soon as it was known here that Sheriff McBride and Deputies Kempton and Wooten had been killed by the Power boys and Sisson, preparations were made at once to send a posse with instructions to get the murderers, dead or alive.

All the while telegrams were sent to the sheriffs of Gila, Cochise, Pima and Greenlee counties, notifying them of the tragedy and to start out posses in pursuit of the murderers, who were believed to be headed for Old Mexico. A posse, headed by Deputy David Skaggs, which included A.G. Walker and Rudd Phillips, left here about 6:00 o'clock Sunday evening, to join a posse already formed and waiting at Klondyke to trail the murderers. About the same time posses were organized at Thatcher, Pima, Fairview and Ft. Thomas and all left at once for Klondyke.

A party was organized here, consisting of Dr. W.E. Platt, W.V. Thorpe, W.R. Chambers, W.W. Pace, Nate Kempton, Frank Webster, Sam Holman, D.H. Claridge and Joe Bleak, for the purposes of going to Klondyke and for bringing the bodies of the slain officers to Safford for an inquest. This party left about o'clock Sunday evening. Later in the evening, Constable Lancaster, Frank Campbell, R.W. Smith and Curley Laffont left Wilcox to join the posse at that place.

Word was received here Sunday night that the murderers were seen near the town of Redington, on the San Pedro River, where they received supplies at the county store. It was the belief here that the Power brothers and Sisson would try and make their way into Old Mexico over an old trail they traveled when they went into Mexico to evade the Selective Service draft last summer.

Posses under Sheriff Harry Wheeler, of Cochise County, Deputy James Hamilton, of Gila County and Sheriff Rye Miles, Sheriff of Pima County were following closely on the trail of the bandits.

Tuesday morning about 3:00 o'clock, W.N. Wilson, Joe Bleak and W.C. Wease, left here in F.I. Ginter's car for Wilcox, with Mr. Ginter driving, to join Sheriff Wheeler's posse. Mr. Ginter returned here about 4:00 o'clock in the afternoon accompanied by Curley Laffont,, who left Sunday night with a posse from Wilcox.

Reports came in Tuesday afternoon stating that the murderers were seen on their way to San Simon. Deputy U.S. Marshal Frank Haynes and Lem R. Pace left at once for San Simon, but found the report to be untrue and returned home. Later reports came in Wednesday morning stating the murderers had been at the Cross X Ranch, where they changed horses, leaving their horses and the mule at the ranch.

Yesterday morning it was reported that they had gotten away from the Cross X Ranch, cutting the barbed wire fence and their trail was headed in the direction of the Chiricahua Mountains. Later yesterday afternoon, another posse left here, headed by Deputies Brig Stewart, Dave Nelson and Leslie Layton, headed to Wilcox to pick up the trail of the murderers and relieve the other possess.

Two troops of U.S. Cavalry were dispatched by Colonel Morgan Wednesday night to patrol the boundary line east of Douglas, with orders to leave the border to aid in the capture of the outlaws if they got across the border into Old Mexico.

Blood hounds were put on the trail of the murderers Tuesday by Sheriff Miles, of Pima County, which followed the trail of the murderers from Cary's ranch, across the San Pedro River and northwest along the San Pedro Valley. It was believed that the murderers had doubled back on the trail Wednesday, as Sheriff Frank Wattron had trailed them within a mile of the store at Redington.

There now are several posses' in the field, totaling over 200 men searching for the outlaws, and are augmented by two U.S. Cavalry troops, patrolling the border, with Mexican troops patrolling the Mexican side. Information came in late Wednesday that the murderers had left Cochise stronghold in the Dragoon Mountains and were tracked on their way to the Chiricahua Mountains. There are a number of draft evaders in these mountains and the Power brothers and Tom Sisson are well aware of and who they will probably join.

Fifteen head of horses were shipped by express on this morning's train, by R.G. Layton, destined for Rodeo, N.M., in charge of Charles Pursley, Jake Felshaw, Howard McBride and Simon Matthews. These horses will be used by the posse from that section to go into the Peloneillo range of the Chiricahua Mountains.

This afternoon word was received from Warren Smith, who is with the posse guarding Busenbacks's ranch, that the murderers' trail has been picked up 25 miles south of Busenback's ranch.

In the same edition of the paper there was another article pertinent to the story about the funeral arrangements for the *slain officers, and resolutions adopted at a mass meeting at the Safford City Hall.*

A mass meeting of citizens and business men was held Tuesday night at the city hall, called by Mayor Jacobson, for the purpose of making arrangements for the joint funeral of slain officers, Mayor Jacobson presided. The citizens in the meeting decided, that all business places in town be closed Wednesday, from 9:30 am to 5:00 pm.

A committee was appointed to secure three motor trucks and decorate them, the trucks to be used in carrying the caskets to Layton Hall for the funeral services and then onto the cemetery for burial. A committee, consisting of Judge A.G. McAlister, Senator D.H. Claridge and Lee N. Stratton was appointed to draw up resolutions which were unanimously adopted by the committee.

Resolutions

We the citizens of the county of Graham, State of Arizona, in a mass meeting assembled at the City Hall in Safford on this 12th day of February, 1918 do hereby adopt the following resolutions:

Whereas on the 10th day of February, 1918, Sheriff R.P. McBride, and deputies Kempton and Wooten were ruthlessly slain by murderous bandits while in the discharge of their official duty in attempting to arrest two evaders of the Selective Service Draft Act.

Whereas, we recognize the fact that they lost their lives while bravely defending the honor of the nation and courageously upholding the law of the land;

Whereas, we further recognize their sterling qualities as public life, and that by their death the County of Graham and the State of Arizona has suffered irreparable loss,

Now, therefore, be it resolved, that we extend to their bereaved families our heartfelt sympathy in this their hour of severest trial, and, that these resolutions be published, and engrossed copies of them be delivered to the wives and children of the deceased.

The bodies of the fallen officers were put in the back of two trucks when the posse reached Klondyke and then they were transported to Safford where the inquest was performed on the following Monday afternoon. The coroner's verdict was that the officers died of gunshot wounds inflicted at the hands of Tom Power, John Power and Tom Sisson.

When the Power brothers and Tom Sisson arrived at Redington it was late afternoon. The sun was setting. A cowboy friend came up to talk with them as they were dismounting. He already knew about the shooting. He told them that Sheriff Rye Miles called Sheriff Harry Wheeler, who said if he caught us we would
not come back alive.

On the next page is a picture of Cochise Stronghold that was found on the hiking.com website and used with their permission. One can see why Cochise chose it for a hideout as well as the Power Brothers and Tom Sisson. It is very rugged and full of hiding places. There is only two ways into this canyon.

Below is another article that appeared in the Graham Guardian Newspaper on February 16th 1918 shedding more information of the pursuit.

Posses Close on Outlaws Trail

Over 200 Men Now Out Following Up Murderers of Officers

Soldiers Guarding the Border

As soon as the bodies of the fallen officers reached the courthouse here in Safford, telegrams were sent to the sheriffs of Gila, Cochise, Pima and Greenlee counties, notifying them of the tragedy and to start out possess in pursuit of the murderers, who were believed to be headed for Old Mexico. A posse headed by Deputy David Skaggs, which included several prominent Safford businessmen, left here at about 6:00 o'clock Sunday evening, to join a posse already formed, and waiting for them in Klondyke to trail the murderers.

About the same time possess were organized and equipped at Thatcher, Pima, Fairview and Ft. Thomas and left at once for Klondyke. Further word was received here Sunday night that the murderers were seen near Redington, on the San Pedro, where they received supplies at a country store. It was their belief there that the Power brothers and Sisson would try to make their way into Old Mexico, over an old trail they traveled in the past.

Posses under Sheriff Wheeler, of Cochise County, Deputy Sheriff Hamilton, of Gila County, and Sheriff Rye Miles, of Pima County were following closely on the tail of the outlaws.

Reports came in Tuesday stating that the murderers had been at Cross X Ranch, where they changed horses, leaving the mule at the ranch. Yesterday it was reported they had got away from the Cross X Ranch, cutting the barbed wire fence, and gong in the direction of the Chiricahua Mountains.

Two troops of U.S. Cavalry were dispatched by Colonel Morgan yesterday to patrol the boundary east of Douglas, with orders to leave the border to aid in the capture of the murderers.

Bloodhounds were put on the trail of the murderers by Sheriff Miles of Pima County, which followed the trail of the murderers from Cary's ranch, across the San Pedro River, and northwest along the San Pedro Valley. It was believed that the murderers had doubled back on the trail, as Frank Wooten had trailed them within a mile of the store at Redington.

A report, received here this morning, indicated that the outlaws camped last night in Cochise Stronghold. Wednesday they had camped in Busenback's pasture, one mile from Dos Cabezas. In leaving the pasture they cut the barbed wire fence. On their way to this point, they had stopped at a farmhouse near Pearce and secured some food for themselves. Men are stationed at all high points in the Dos Cabezas Mountains and are sweeping the country around with field glasses.

There are now in posses over 200 men and this force is augmented by the two troops of U.S. Cavalry, patrolling the border, with Mexican troops also patrolling the Mexican side of the border also alerted to look for the outlaws. Later information arrived indicating the murderers had gone from the Cochise Stronghold in the Dragoon Mountains to the Chiricahuas. There are a number of draft evaders known to be in those mountains, a fact which the Power brothers and Sisson are surely aware of and it is thought that they are trying to join the slackers now camped in those mountains.

Several head of horses were shipped to Dos Cabezas so the posse would have fresh mounts before continuing their chase. This afternoon word was received here from Warren Smith, who is with the posse guarding Busenback's ranch, that the murderers' trail has been picked up again at a point 25 miles south of the

Busenback's ranch.

Tom Power picks up the story again stating;

> *"We decided our best bet would be to head for Old Mexico. We would be safe from the law down there."*

The next morning a Tuesday according to Tom;

> *"Our day started before daylight."*

He went on to say that he and John were both broken up about their father being shot. Their main concern had been about him. After his death, when they rode by Mahoney's place on their way to Redington, they were in no shape to talk over the circumstances surrounding the shootout. Both John and Tom were in tremendous pain due to the fact that they both lost an eye in the gunfight and John had most of his nose blown off. They both had glass and wood splinters in their faces, eyes and our upper bodies from the glass and wood sprinters. After the shootout according to Tom, when they walked the property and recognized two of the three bodies as law officers, but they had no idea why the officers had come after them. They knew, because the dead men were officers of the law that it was not safe for them to stay at the mine. But honestly they had no idea how much trouble they were in until they talked to their cowboy friend.

Tom Power went on to say that, his brother John and Tom Sisson mounted their horses and hit the road right after they ate breakfast. After they rode the trail toward Old Mexico for about two hours they ran into a truck with a rack bed that had a lot of men standing up in the bed and hanging onto the rack. These men were part of several posses that had already formed to catch them. The truck went right past them. Tom said they went across the road and into the San Pedro River. He said they watered their horses, filled their canteens and took a little rest. Tom said then they traveled down the river for a few miles to a point where they saw some large meadows. They turned their horses loose so they could graze and they went ahead and slept there for the night.

The next day Tom said they traveled towards the town of Cochise. Tom Sisson led them because he was familiar with the country having scouted the area and pursuing renegade Apaches while he was in the Army. That evening they came to a ranch where there was a huge haystack, a large water tank, and some stock around it. They rested for an hour allowing their horses to feed and drink. Then they caught a bay gelding and traded it for the sorrel mule. Tom said they mounted the horses and rode through the night until they reached the railroad tracks southeast of Cochise and followed the railroad tracks a few miles, crossed under a bridge, and from there they headed toward the Cochise Stronghold. As they reached a mountain peak they studied the surrounding for long ways since it was a bright, clear day. The men took turns sleeping that night, but stayed on the mountain the next day and watched their back trail. However, there seemed to be no one looking for them. That evening they headed to the town of Pearce, Arizona and stopped at a house where they bought some food. Tom states;

> "The people in the house were very nice but as soon as we left, they called the authorities to report we had been there and left. An alarm had been put out for us over the whole countryside."

On the next page at two newspaper articles that were published in the Tucson Daily Star on February 12th and 13th of 1918, that bear out facts about Sheriff Miles' posse chasing the outlaws into Cochise Stronghold.

Sheriff Miles Drives Slayers of McBride into Stronghold of Cochise: Holds Them at Bay

Tucson Sheriff, Exhausted, Had Quarry Bagged Last Night in Lair of Old Indian Chief, and waiting on U.S. Cavalry in Pursuit

Douglas, Feb. 12---Colonel George H. Morgan, commander of the Arizona military district, tonight dispatched two troops of cavalry to patrol the International boundary east of Douglas to prevent Tom and John Power and Tom Sisson, Graham county slayers of Sheriff McBride and two deputies last Sunday morning, from escaping into Old Mexico. These troops have orders to leave the border patrol if it is thought by doing so they can aid in the capture of the men. Colonel Morgan said tonight to this reporter that the International line would be carefully guarded to keep the fugitives from crossing.

Whether the Powers-Sisson gang are making their way back to the scene of the gunfight, or whether they have broken through the cordon of man-hunters bent upon their capture, will become evident this afternoon when Sheriff Miles with a posse, trailing through the broken country east of the San Pedro river, northward from Benson, reaches the Power's ranch.

Reinforcements: Four Posses on the Way from Bisbee: U.S. Cavalry Guards Border to Prevent Possible Escape

Bisbee, Ariz., Feb. 13-Entirely played out and waiting reinforcements, Sheriff Miles of Pima County, drove Tom and John Powers and Tom Sisson into Cochise Stronghold, a formidable natural barrier located about 10 miles west of Pearce Arizona. Four posses are being sent out of Bisbee to guard the southern edge of the stronghold and the sheriff's office is sending out men to take care of the western side of the mountains. From Johnson, Gleason, Pearce and Wilcox posses are also in action.

Sheriff Miles picked up the trail of the murderers late this afternoon and followed it across the Southern Pacific tracks between Johnson and Cochise. He was but a short time behind the men when they went into the mountains.

Chief Deputy Sheriff Guy Welch of Tombstone is on his way to Gleason, near Cochise Stronghold, and should arrive after midnight tonight. He is to take charge of the several posses in that area. He plans to split up his organizations and station the men along the west, east and southern side of the Dragoon Mountains, in which the stronghold is located. With Sheriff Rye Miles of Pima County, and officers from Johnson, Pearce, Cochise and Wilcox, on the northern side of the mountains, hope is expressed that the murderers will be either apprehended or killed.

Cochise Stronghold, where the three murderers of the Graham officers are said to have taken refuge, is one of the great natural forts in the southwest. It was made famous and named after the Apache chief, Cochise, who terrorized southeastern Arizona in the 1870's. It was this stronghold that Cochise, in July of 1871, drove a herd of cattle stolen near Fort Bowie, that Captain Jerry Russell and his troops of the Third cavalry were ambushed and all but wiped out by Cochise, when the army officer and his troops attempted to get into the barrier.

Below is the first article that appeared regarding the pursuit of the Power gang that appeared in the Silver Belt Newspaper that was published in Globe, Arizona on February 12, 1918;

Below is another article that was published in the Silver Belt Newspaper the following day, February 13, 1918 regarding the pursuit of the Power gang;

McBride Slayers near Pool, Report from Authorities

Wanted Men Said to be on Way to Happy Valley and Possess Are Closing in: Battle seems Near

Tucson, Feb. 13- At 10 o'clock tonight word was received at the sheriff's office here that John and Tom Powers and Thomas Sisson, slayers of Sheriff McBride of Graham county and two of his deputies, Kempton and Wooten are in the vicinity of Pool, southwest of Redington, where they had earlier been reported, and are moving toward Happy Valley, where Sheriff Miles of Pima county is stationed with a strong posse of crack shots. Sheriff Harry Wheeler of Cochise County is closing in from Benson and another posse will leave

Fuller's Pass at daybreak to participate in the pursuit.

Both Sheriff Miles and Sheriff Wheeler were members of the old territorial Arizona Rangers, and are experts in man-hunting. Practically every expert rifle shot's in Tucson have joined one or the other of the posses'.

Governor Hunt today offered a reward of $3,000 for the capture, dead or alive, of the three men. Graham County has also added a reward of $1,000. An additional $3,000 reward by the federal government has been added to the reward bringing the total reward for the capture of the murderers to $7,000 dead or alive.

Below is a photo of the wanted poster for the capture of the Power gang, that was sent to every law officer in Arizona and New Mexico.

The pursuit of the Power brothers and Tom Sisson proved unique in several ways. Not only the sheer numbers of men participating in the hunt, the intensity of feelings generated over a period of almost a month, but the fact this hunt eclipsed all previous undertakings in Arizona history.

While horses were the predominant means of transportation, the manhunt bridged the eras of early west and the new west, using sophisticated equipment and highly trained personnel. The automobile rapidly changing the complexion of our society also played part in hauling equipment and supplies, and helped in the rapid deployment of men into the field.

The most dramatic evidence of the transition from the hard-riding, fast-shooting sheriffs to lawmen of the new era was the use of the airplane. Horses in law enforcement faded fast from the picture after this manhunt, in which airplanes were used for the first time in aviation history in the pursuit of criminals.

Tom Power continues the story; It was very dark when we reached Pearce. Two cars came along the road in front of us just before we reached the town. We crossed the railroad tracks using the light from their vehicles. We learned later that Frank Wooten, the brother of deceased Kane Wooten was in the lead car. We were blinded by their car lights and at the insistence of Mr. Sisson, who thought he knew the area, we got on the wrong road by turning north instead of south. To his defense it was very dark and we could hardly see in front of us as we road slowly down the road. At Chiricahua West Well, we came upon a large posse. It consisted of trucks, cars and horses. The men had built a fire, and had lighted lanterns around their camp. Three of them were standing guard wide-eyed, sleeping with their eyes open. We know this because we snuck into their camp to get warm and eat some left-over beans still warm in the pot. Still sleeping, no one made any effort to pursue us.

We headed for the mining town of Dos Cabezas, but stopped to sleep and wait for daylight. In the morning we realized Dos Cabezas was still quite a long way off and headed south toward the Chiricahuas. In the evening, we saw a car coming down the road toward us loaded with men. Guns were sticking out on each side of the car. I saw the car turn left off the road about 200 yards from us. Thankfully the posse did not see us and we continued on to the foot of the mountains, where we stopped and ate our dinner. There was a spring nearby and a lot of good grass for the horses to graze. We got a good nights' sleep.

The next morning after sunup, doves came into our camp, cooing and fluttering all around us. It was a beautiful experience. We proceeded up a mountain trail nearby and found a great spot at the top of the ridge that allowed us to gaze back along the valley trail with field glasses. It wasn't long before we spotted four men on horseback looking for sign. Our horses were getting pretty leg weary; having been ridden for many days and nights. We didn't want to kill anyone; we had our fill of killing, but we knew if we stayed with the horses, there would be a gun battle and more killing would happen. We rode quickly to a canyon close by and turned our horses loose. We backtracked over the ridge, the way we had come, and down a steep hill into the next canyon. We hoped this maneuver would throw the trackers off our trail just long enough so they could get away. While going down the hill, we replaced our boots and put on our shoes. It was too difficult to walk any farther in our boots. Soon we crossed some slick rocks and found a nice stream, wading to the other side we stopped to drink and fill our canteens.

Later in the day we headed up the side of a canyon. We traveled south to the far side, found a fence crawled under and crossed a road. We rested in that little canyon, some 50 to 70 yards from the road. That evening, we heard people going by our camp in cars and on horseback. I overheard one man say;

> "We will go up there and cut them off tonight."

I realized at that point the posse thought we were still up on the ridge so we headed up to the top a hill well south of where the posse was camped. We continued walking south to another canyon about three or four miles away and found a spot where we thought it would be safe to stay and sleep the night. After eating a cold breakfast, we climbed up to the top of the first high mountain in the Chiricahua mountain range. It was covered with snow. We crossed a little canyon and turned south. We traveled all that day until we got to a mesa where there were lots of pine trees. We gathered up pine needles and made ourselves beds where we spent the night. We covered our bodies with pine needles, bear grass and tree limbs to keep ourselves warm. It was cold but thankfully we were out of the snow. The next morning, we continued heading south toward our ultimate goal, the Mexican border. Tom said;

> "We came to a fork in the trail, we took the fork to the left that went up over a ridge. Tom Sisson told us he was not sure which trail to take but he guessed the left one would get us to our destination the fastest. We discovered later that we made the right choice; had we gone down the other trail we would have run smack dab into a posse that was waiting for us."

Later in the afternoon when we stopped for a rest we saw nine cavalry soldiers ride nearby as they were patrolling the canyon. After they left we walked down into the canyon and found a good stream. We took off our shoes and waded in the creek. We filled our canteens and rested there for a couple of hours until it was dark before continuing our trek.

It was a beautiful clear night, almost a full moon and the sky bright stars. Sisson was familiar with the country having scouted the Apaches when he was in the Army. He wanted to take advantage of the well-lit sky and the fact that our trackers would be sleeping. Since we were on foot we needed any advantage we could muster. At daylight the next morning we climbed a mountain. At the top we found a nice area with pine trees and rested there on beds of pine needles for a few hours.

Late in afternoon we traveled down the other side of the mountain. At the bottom we crossed into a canyon that ran north and south, but headed east and kept going until we reached a peak in the Chiricahua Mountains overlooking the town of Rodeo, New Mexico. It started raining, but got colder; the rain turned to snow. We built a lean-to out of pine logs, bear grass, and brush. We stayed there under the protection of the lean-to for one day and two nights. We were in dire need of rest and we knew the rain and snow would obliterate our tracks. The snow allowed us to stay put and rest without worrying about our trackers finding us. We could see the possess patrolling in the valley far below us. We left the lean-to when we ran out of food; although we were cold we were well rested and had no fear of being caught.

We went down the other side of the canyon again toward Rodeo. We circled around a posse camped in the canyon watering their animals. We passed close enough to hear the men laughing and talking. We stayed hidden until they had passed. We followed the canyon down to a large wide opening and spotted a ranch where a bunch of the posse was camped. Some dogs barked at us, but no one came out. We circled the place and went on for a few miles until we reached some railroad tracks. We saw where a large patrol had beaten out quite a path; we crossed among these tracks to hide our progress.

Chapter Eleven

The civilian officers that came to take us to Safford were Brig Stewart, the new Sheriff of Graham County; Mack McCarthy, a Deputy Marshal of town of Duncan, Arizona; Sheriff Frank Shriver of Silver City, New Mexico and Sheriff John Slaughter of Greenlee County. Lieutenant Hayes took them to Hachita, New Mexico for the night. The Commanding officer at the post called Washington, D.C., to find out what to do with the prisoners. Officials in Washington wired back that there were no federal charges against Tom and John Power for not registering for the draft or any other reason. The wire indicated this was because Arizona's draft quota was complete. The wire indicated that the sheriffs would have to proceed with any arrests for any state or local charges or the army would turn the outlaws loose.

Sheriff Shriver lobbied with the army commander in Hachita to take us to his jail in Silver City, New Mexico based on the fact that they were caught in Southeastern, New Mexico. The sheriff told the army commander that the murderers would be held in his jail until the New Mexico governor signed extradition papers to have the outlaws moved to Safford for trial.

This plan was Sheriff Shriver's intention from the start. An article appeared in the Graham Guardian the day the men were captured indicating that Sheriff Shriver was the officer that captured us. The army commander happened to read the article and realized it was a stunt so Shriver could collect the $7,000 reward. The commander said he would only release men to Arizona officers.

This Article appeared in the same edition of the Graham examiner on March 12th, 1918.

Sheriff Shriver Claims Capture
Frank Schriver, sheriff of Grand County, N.M., has been wrongfully

*credited with the capture of the outlaws,
John and Tom Power along with Tom
Sisson in a dramatic article in the El Paso
Times.*

*We understand that the valiant sheriff
claims the reward offered for the capture
of the outlaws. The facts are that the
outlaws were captured by the U.S.
Cavalry-men and were turned over to
Sheriff Stewart by the commanding officer
at the army base in Hachita N.M., Captain
Mitchell, and Sheriff Schriver was
nowhere in sight at the time of the
capture.*

Before turning the outlaws over to the custody of
the state and local officers Lieutenant Hayes made
three civilian lawmen sign a paper stating that they
would protect the accused outlaws with their lives,
and would not let anyone harm us. This action was
taken because he saw a mob of 30 people outside
the prison walls looking to lynch us if possible. Hayes
told the civilian officers after releasing us into their
custody that if any harm came to us on the way to
stand trial in Safford that he would bring his whole
army to Safford and there would be severe prices to
pay. The civilian authorities loaded us into a car with
three officers and a young man that was the chauffer
for the trip to Safford. Four other officers followed us
in another vehicle to protect us on the long ride from
Hachita, N.M. to Safford, some 300 miles.

The caravan arrived at Duncan, Arizona about
dinner time, which was about halfway between
Hachita, N.M. and Safford, AZ. The officers decided
to spend the night there and take off in the morning to
complete the trip to Safford. We spent the night in the
local city jail, where the town marshal was told to
keep it quiet that we were being held there. We were
given food that evening but as I said;

"Not enough to fill us up."

However, a little later Mack McCarthy, one of the deputies and his wife brought us plenty of good food. Mack and his wife lived in Duncan.

Even though nobody was supposed to know we were being held, the next morning, I saw there was a large crowd gathered to get a look at us as we were transferred to the awaiting vehicles to take us to Safford. McCarthy and Sheriff Stewart pushed the crowd out of the way as they started pressing to get a closer to us. Sheriff Slaughter and Shriver held onto us and guided us to the vehicles. One old man began cursing the officers. Deputy McCarthy shouted out;

> *"People! These three men are all friends of mine, so get out of the way before we have to start using our night sticks to clear a path."*

When we finally arrived in Safford just before dinner and were taken into the sheriff's office and led upstairs to the jail. Even though the officers took the back way into town another large crowd had gathered to watch the cars bring us in. It was impossible to avoid being seen by towns' people as word had spread throughout the state that we were being transported to Safford.

Below are a couple syndicated articles that were published in the Arizona Daily Star on Tuesday March 14th, 1918;

SAFFORD JAIL IS LOCKED ON POWERS GANG

Murderers of Sheriff McBride Are Turned by Soldiers Over to State Authorities; Thomas Powers Has Wounded Left Eye

Safford, Ariz., March 10. John Power, Thomas Power and Thomas Sisson, who were captured yesterday by an American cavalry patrol eight miles south of the Mexican border, were brought here late today by Sheriff Stewart of Graham county, and looked in a cell in the county jail to await trial on a charge of killing three Graham county officers on February 10th of this year.

All three of the prisoners are footsore and weary and Thomas Powers is suffering from a wound in the left eye, which may necessitate its removal. The wound was received in the gunfight on February 10th, when the three officers, who sought to arrest the Power brothers as alleged draft evaders, were killed.

Another article that was published in the Silver Belt newspaper out of Globe, Arizona on March, 14, 1918;

Outlaws Moved Secretly

Globe, Ariz., March 10--Tom Sisson along with Tom and John Power were taken from Hachita here to Safford and arrived at about 4 o'clock this afternoon secretly in automobiles and under heavy guard. They were immediately placed in the county jail, where they will be held until it is determined whether they will be charged with murder under the state or federal laws. They are the slayers of Sheriff Frank McBride and his deputies Mart Kempton and Kane Wooten. In the event that they are tried and convicted on first degree murder under the state laws, the anti-capital punishment act in Arizona will save them from execution by the state.

The prisoners are indifferent to their fate, according to a telephone message from R.W. Smith, Clerk of the Superior Court of

Graham County. The only regret they expressed was over the death of Kempton. They said that they thought the man to be Howard McBride, the brother but they freely admitted that they did not recognize Kempton at first. They went on to say that they did recognize Kane Wooten and Sheriff McBride. Tom said that he and John were shocked when they discovered one of the men they shot was Sheriff McBride, who they considered a good friend from campaigning for him and selling bootleg liquor for him several years ago. They said they were not shocked that one of the dead men was Kane Wooten because they knew there had been friction between them and the Wooten family.

Three Sheriffs Guard Trio

Guarding the prisoners on their trip here from Hachita were Sheriff Stewart the new sheriff of Graham County, Sheriff Schiber of Grant County, and Undersheriff Carl Foster also of Graham County. A demonstration against the men was feared, but the people of Safford restrained themselves, and it was stated at a late hour that there was little fear of lynching.

The shooting rose over the fact that Deputy United States Marshal Frank Haynes of Globe, assisted by the slain Graham County officers, sought to arrest the two Power boys as draft evaders. Sisson aided the youths to fight the officers as did their father, who was killed in the battle that occurred at their mountain home in Rattlesnake Canyon,

Prisoners Talk Freely

The prisoners talked freely about their flight from the lawmen numbering more than two thousand men. They said that they were on foot from the time they abandoned their victims' horses between Rock Creek Canyon and Turkey Creek on Friday, February 16th, six days after the battle. When they left their cabin they made straight from Turkey Creek across Cottonwood Canyon to Prieden Canyon, the head of which they crossed. Then they said they crossed the head of Rucker Canyon and on into the head of Horseshoe Canyon, where they camped for four days. Crossing the San Simon they entered Skeleton Canyon, where Sisson formerly owned a ranch. Skeleton Canyon is in the Guadalupe Mountains in the southeast border of New Mexico and Arizona. From that point they made their way south, going by Hachita and crossing the border into Old Mexico. Unable to find food and water as well as not being familiar with the territory they decided to turn back toward the border and the only water they knew which was a well eight miles south of the border in Mexico where they were captured.

After making sure that the boys were secured in separate jail cells, washed and fed, they opened the doors so the people could see the outlaws and know they were safely confined. People lined up for several hundred yards walking in single file past the murderers to see first hand that they were in jail and well guarded. People filed by their cell for a good two hours. Tom said it seemed like everyone in the county wanted to see them. He said that there must have been five hundred people come in to file past their cells to get a good look at them.

Several critical situations developed shortly after the men were logged in the Safford jail. The first occurred when a close relative of one of the slain officers came in that first evening. Deputy Dave Skaggs, the jailer, was close by, and knowing the bitterness of the bereaved relatives, watched the man intently. When the man started up the stairs Skaggs followed and recounted:

I watched him step inside the room where the Power brothers and Sisson were jailed. He stood looking at them for several minutes through the cell bars. I guess the fact that Sisson lolled against the bars with his leering face almost touching them, was too much for my friend. Suddenly I realized his hand was on his gun. I wasn't absolutely sure of his arms to his sides. He had no idea who had accosted him so he wrestled around with me until we both stumbled down the short flight of stairs to the room below. His gun was still in his pocket as we confronted each other. With a strange look in his eye he finally said;

"By God, Dave you are still a friend of mine' then he pulled off his hat to wipe away the sweat that beaded his forehead, then added, 'this is no place for me' then he turned on his heel and left."

Another incident had also taken place at that time was Deputy Sheriff Lancaster became involved in a situation which could have had dire results had it not been for his quick decision and tact. An ordeal involving some of his excited friends, who felt duty-bound to take justice into their own hands, were rumored to be forming a lynching party. As Lancaster was leaving the jail, Sheriff Stewart, stopped Deputy Lancaster at the door. He told him about the rumors. Instead of going home, Lancaster volunteered to wander around town to see what could be learned.

He hoped to be able to talk to those who might be involved, then he came upon his first prospect in a poolroom, where a relative of one of the decease officer's approached Deputy Lancaster and said;

> "I hear you are planning a lynching party."

The other man, equally frank, replied;

> "That's right, and I don't mind you knowing it."

Lancaster tried to reason with, telling him he knew how bitter he felt, but if he and his friends would let the law take its course, he would not be sorry. He pointed out that if they tried to lynch the boys, they would regret it and that to hang the boys would make them murderers too. The lynching was avoided.

Deputy Dave Skaggs contacted one of the supervisors about new clothes, for the three prisoners as they had arrived filthy, unshaven, hair matted, with their clothes dirty and torn. He soon realized he must attend to this himself, for the supervisor said;

> "To hell with them. I wouldn't care if their asses were on the ground."

The khaki pants and shirts which Dave purchased gave him considerable satisfaction, and eventually the city board did compensate him for the expenditures. He also took it upon himself to send for Doc Warner to come check Tom and John's eyes. That same evening, a Safford barber, Tom Naylor, gave the prisoners a shave and cut their hair. This made them a little more presentable to the huge, milling throng of curious people who jammed the jail, eager to glimpse the notorious murderers. Tom and John continued to say little, but Sisson appeared to enjoy all the attention.

Tom and John were very familiar with Doc Warner as he was one of the doctors who had treated their sister for back and neck problems. The first thing Warner did was look at Tom's eye. He noted some glass fragments in the left eye, but he did not have the right equipment with him to correctly treat the eye. However, he went ahead and removed the larger pieces of glass and cleaned up the eye. He also treated John's eye by removing all of the wood splinters that he could see with the naked eye. He gave John a solution of cocaine and morphine to deaden the intense pain he was enduring.

The doctor came back a second time to treat John's eye and applied a solution to prevent infection. John said the solution caused such incredible intense pain that he could not see anything being totally blind in the treated eye. To make things worse the jail guard took away John's pain medication but Mr. Sisson and Tom Power raised so much commotion; Sheriff Slaughter returned the pain medicine.

Attorney James S. Fielder, a longtime friend of Jeff Power, came to represent us from Deming, New Mexico. Charlie Power had read about the gunfight and his brothers' capture in the national news; he paid Fielder a retainer fee and sent him to represent his brothers. Charlie never came to see them but Tom and John understood Charlie wanted no part of their world. However, we were very thankful that he showed us brotherly love.

Many times in the past we had heard our father tell of Attorney Fielder's uncanny ability to sway juries and obtain miraculous acquittals when all seemed lost; naturally our hopes were pinned on this New Mexico spellbinder.

We were in jail a couple days when a troop of 800 soldiers came through Safford, travelling from Miami to Douglas. The soldiers came by the jail to see us, then brought their commanding officer back with them. The commanding officer asked us a few questions, and specifically if we were the men the army captured and released to the civilian officers who had signed an agreement to protect us. I said we were the men in question. We were surprised when he simply told us good luck and left the jail with his soldiers.

A crowd of people was gathered on one of the street corners near the jail and were threatening to lynch us. As he departed the jail the commanding officer walked up to the lynch mob and told them he didn't want to hear anymore talk about lynching. He warned them;

> *"I'll be stationed in Douglas, and I'll be in charge of the closest soldiers. If anything happens to those three boys in jail, I'll come back here and clean this valley up, so you'd all better break up and go home."*

The next two moves by our attorney, James Fielder was first, to waive the right to a preliminary hearing. Next he petitioned the court to move the trial to the Superior Court of Greenlee County, located in Clifton, due to the fact that his clients would not get a fair trial in Graham County. The court granted to move the trial. We were taken to Clifton by Sheriff Stewart and lodged in the county jail to await trial.

A news article that was published in the Tucson Daily Star on March 16th 1918;

Murders Granted Change of Venue

Tucson, AZ-John and Tom Power along with Tom Sisson, charged with the murder of Sheriff McBride and his Deputies Kempton and Wooten, February 10th, who were captured. March 8th, in Mexico, by U.S. cavalrymen were brought here to Clifton to be held for trial. Sheriff Brig Stewart has them confined in the Greenlee County jail here in Clifton. Their arraignment was last Wednesday in front of Judge McAlister in the Greenlee County Superior Court. At that time, they pleaded not guilty on all charges. Their trial date has been set for May 13th 1918.

Below is a photo found in our National Archives of the Greenlee County Courthouse where the trial of the Power brothers and Tom Sisson took place. It is in the county capital city of Clifton, Arizona

Chapter Twelve

The trial of John and Tom Power along with Tom Sisson started on May 13th 1918 and took place at the Greenlee County Courthouse in Clifton, Arizona. The presiding judge was Frank B. Laine. The prosecution team was comprised of David Ling of Greenlee County; District Attorney W.R. Chambers of Graham County, who had conducted the inquest, and Norman Johnson of Globe. In his opening statement W.R. Chambers presented a double-action pistol with belt and scabbard into evidence that was believed to belong to the Power brothers. Tom said they had never seen these items before the trial.

At that point prosecutor Ling approached the bench and withdrew from the prosecution team. He told the judge he would not work with Chambers and Johnson because he was not comfortable with their ethics.

The Power brothers and Tom Sisson's attorney, James Fielder, was involved with the jury selection questioning each juror to be sure that they had not heard about the shootout and to make sure they would not be biased jurors. There were 33 men interviewed and the selection of 12 jurors was complete by four o'clock that afternoon. The court was recessed with the trial to be continued the next day May 14th, 1918.

The trial transcripts along with most of the legal records have all disappeared or have been misplaced over the years. The only record of the trial is the one that was obtained by Charlie Power within a couple of weeks right after the end of the trial, but now even that record has disappeared or has been misplaced. Below is the record of the trial recorded by Tom Power.

The first witness to take the stand for the state was U.S. Deputy Marshal Frank Haynes, who was sworn in to take the oath that everything he said was the truth, the whole truth, and nothing but the truth The Graham County Attorney, W.R. Chambers was the man asking the questions, and Haynes written testimony follows. Charlie Power was able to get a copy of the trial records before they mysteriously disappeared from the records department in the basement of the courthouse in Clifton and also from the records department in the basement of the Graham County courthouse as well. The author was told that there was a fire in the basement of the Clifton and curiously a fire in the basement of the Graham County courthouse. The nature of these fires is very dubious, putting it mildly. One has to wonder if the powers to be were trying to Q. *What official position do you hold the United States Government?*

    A. Deputy United States Marshal.
    Q. For what district?
    A. District of Northeastern Arizona.
    Q. Did you have occasion to come to
        Safford about the 8th or 9th of
        February, this past year for the
        purpose of getting
        some assistance to go out to the
        Galiuro Mountains to arrest some
        slackers?
    Q. All right. What did you do, when you?
        came to Safford, with reference to
        making the arrangements?
    A. Well, the arrangements were to have
        been made by Mr. McBride, that we
        arranged by mail, and when I come
        down Mr. McBride didn't know
        whether now would be the best time
        to go up there or not. He was
        interested in court that day. That was
        Thursday, February the 7th. Friday he

was able to obtain the warrants. We stayed around Safford while McBride arranged for two men to hide something; join us to serve the warrants. Saturday morning Sheriff McBride and I left with deputies Mart Kempton and Kane Wooten. I had authority from the U.S Marshal to arrange for one posse member and McBride had the authority from the marshal to also take one posse member, who McBride decided decided would be Kane Wooten.

Q. *You only had authority to get one man on your responsibility?*

A. *Yes, sir. I had the warrants for the Power boys, and Mr. McBride had a warrant for old man Power and Sission. Mr. McBride first said he was figuring on getting Johnny Sanford to go with us, but he said Mart Kempton, his Under Sheriff, wanted to go awful bad, and maybe he could arrange for Mart to go. When we were ready to leave, Mr. McBride didn't have the warrants ready and we had to go over to the courthouse and get them. We got away from here about three o'clock. We stopped at Mr. Upchurch's place at Klondyke. It seems that Mr. Wooten had some interest there; he was interested in their ranch. There we got horses and we had our dinner there about six o'clock I guess or later. I don't know what time we left, but it was good and dark when the four of us left there. Kane Wooten was riding a big brown horse and the under-sheriff was riding a sorrel horse. I was riding a white horse and Frank McBride was riding a mule. I didn't know the country but we started out over the trail and we followed that trail until we come to a little ranch house, but there wasn't anybody at home. So we went on up above there a short ways and built a fire. I don't remember what time of night we stopped but we morning. We decided it would take us until daylight to reach the place where we expected to find the Power boys. We rode on up the canyon then until Kane Wooten stopped and said he thought we was pretty close to the place. It was still dark down in the canyon, awful dark; of course, it was a starlit night. He went on to say it had been five or six years since he was up there but he thought we were close to the place. McBride says we had better be a little late than too early. I guess we killed time there for about thirty minutes, and by that time it began to get light, so we rode on. T.K Wooten was riding in front and pretty soon he stopped. He says, there's a house over there, he says, What do you think about it?" Sheriff McBride says, "It's pretty dark to tackle it." One of the boy's say's that the dogs might bay at us. We went to that house and there wasn't anybody there. We got on our horses and beat it over to the old saloon and there was nobody there. We got on our horses again and went up the canyon a short ways and we struck the trail. We had just got on that trail with Kane still in front, and he stopped us and said it didn't seem to look like it was the right trail, but after he studied a minute he says this must be a new trail. The brush was cut along there, like it had been done recently. He says, we will take the new trail. When we got up the heavy grade and turned down the other side, we rode on a little-ways, down and come in sight of a camp. Then Kane said something about crossing over the ridge. We were on the same side of the ridge that the cabin was on. He was thinking of taking advantage of the ridge and coming around the point to the house; then he says, "I believe we are just as well to ride right up there." So we rode within about 75 rods of the house. There is a little side canyon coming down off this ridge and the trail coming down a steep place for probably 75 feet swung around in this little canyon and turned down coming right near the house. Kane Wooten rode off of the trail there and says, we will leave our horses here. We got off of our horses and we pulled off our overcoat's, I cannot say if Kane did, but Frank McBride and Mart Kempton and I pulled off our overcoat's and Mart had on a pair of leather leggings that belonged to Mr. Upchurch or that is where he threw them anyway, after he pulled them off. When we left the trail, Frank McBride and I went off of the trail to the first end of the house and as we approached the house, Mart and Kane stayed on the trail, which*

took them along down by the side of
the house next to the bank, and
around the end of the opposite corner
of the house. Well, just as Frank
McBride and I come to the corner and
before I could see anybody, I heard a
voice I took to be Kane Wooten holler,
"Throw up your hands!"

Q. Could you see him then?
A. No, sir, not the first time. He hollered
again and that time I seen him.
Q. Did he holler three times?
A. Yes. I think he hollered it three times,
but I know he hollered twice, and I
think he hollered twice after Frank
McBride and I come in sight. Frank
and Mart was past the corner that they
had come up to, some four or five feet
on the side of the house, the side next
to the creek. It seemed to me when we
turned down there we were going due
north, but I am informed that we
going just the opposite direction. But
then I didn't see, this one man is the
only man I seen, and Frank McBride
says, "Boys, boys, boys!" Just like that
Then I realized that there was a man in
The door and that he had a Winchester
Q. Did you see him?
A. Yes, sir. I was a thick door jamb it
looked to me, though it wasn't as light
there as it was outside. I would not
recognize the man if I saw him again
. He was in the door way. This door
hinged on the side of towards Mr.
McBride and I. Just when that opened
there were four or five shots, all in a
bunch. The first shots come from the

house. This old man fell. Frank and I
hadn't fired yet, and then Frank
McBride and I then both fired into this
door.

Q. Into the door?

A. Yes, we both fired through the door at
this man inside with the gun. I could
see the gun and his two hands. The
barrel of the gun was fast to the door
shutter.

Q. Did you see him when he fired?

A. I could just see the opening in the
door It looked to me like about that
wide (indicating) that the door was
open. This man fired at us. The first
shot went down low and struck in the
ground. The next shot hit something
above us. I don't know what. We fired
again, and the man in the door-it
looked to me he had turned his gun
right over this way (indicating) with his
hands out of the door and fired
towards Kane Wooten and Mart
Kempton. He turned it over and back
again; there was two shots but I think
that either one of those shot took
effect. Kane Wooten and Mart went
behind that corner of the house and
Frank McBride and I to the other
corner.

Q. You Saw them after the shooting
began, did you?

A. Yes, sir.

Q. Saw both Tim and Mart after the
shooting?

A. Yes, sir. These first shots all come in a
bunch; then there had been four shots
fired after that before they went

behind the corner of the house. Well, Mack and I had arranged that if anything tightened up there, to take the corners of the house Mack motioned to me and I say, "Shall I get to the other corner?" He said, "Yes." I went to the other corner of the house from Mack. I could see Mack from there and I see that there was a window in the end of the house next to us. There was a window in the side of the house? next to the bank, but I couldn't see into those windows, couldn't see anything on the inside at all. Well, I realized then the noise had ceased or slackened up on the other corner of the house and I asked Frank where Kane was and he didn't answer me. Then I backed off a little further from the corner. There was some boards nailed up there on some posts at the end of the house where McBride and I was, they didn't run to the ground and I see McBride still on the corner. He fired two shots from that corner, it might have been three, then I didn't see McBride. Everything was as quiet as could be in the mean time somebody had fired a shot that I thought come out of the window from the end of the house where we were. It hit these boards. I turned around, turned my gun over and fired to that window. Mack was still up then. Then the next thing I realized I couldn't see McBride. I walked down by the side of these boards towards the creek and McBride was laying right on his back with his left leg stretched straight out and his left arm right down by the side of his leg and the other leg was drawn up. I don't know whether it was laying over on the ground that way or whether it was drawn up kind of under him. I was afraid to go around that corner far enough to see McBride's face. I missed the old man out in the yard and I supposed they dragged him in the house. I went back to this other corner and from there I couldn't see McBride's face. I backed off into a kind of a little ravine that comes down at the end of the house where McBride and I was and I couldn't find any place to get any shelter there. I couldn't hear anything. I went up on the trail and I couldn't see nor hear anything there. Then I went up to where, we had left our horses, and. I went up that little steep pitch of the trail that come down to where we had left them horses. I could see anything there. I went to the horses and got on the horse I had ridden and rode straight up the ridge to the top and over into the bushes and I tied him there. Then I struck a trail that I thought would take me far enough down to where I could see the end of the house where the chimney was and where I had seen Kane Wooten and Mart Kempton, but I see I couldn't get down there without getting right back down on the same trail that went right near to the end of the house. I got up in the brush and I looked over and seen somebody in the bushes on the *opposite side. I thought at first it might be Kane Wooten. Then I realized that Wooten either was wearing a Mackinaw and an overcoat over it, and I don't know yet whether Wooten pulled off his overcoat or not. So I couldn't see nor hear anything; then I made up my mind that the best thing I could do was to get back to the settlement and get more help. I followed that old trail and it led me around the opposite side of the ridge from this and took me off into the main canyon right at the corner of what they term the "saloon." It was after eight o'clock and I come on into Klondyke just as fast as I could come. The first man I met there was Johnny Sanford. I told Johnny what had happened to Frank and told him I didn't know whether. Kane and Mart was killed or not. I went on down then to Mr. Upchurch's and was going to get Frank McBride's automobile to raise the Alarm there in the settlement, but Frank had the key and I couldn't start the machine. Johnny come on down and he went on horse someplace. He told me he was going to Klondyke. In the mean-time there was a gentleman come there, he was a member of Board of Supervisors. I didn't know him He had a young fellow there to fix this car so that we could run it without the key. Just about that time this young man, Allen came down and told me that Mart and Kane were both dead.*

Q. How many shots did you fire in there?

do you remember?

A. *I fired three shots. I don't remember whether I fired any more or not.*

Q. *Was that at the door where you fired?*

A. *I fired two shots at the door.*

Q. *And the other one in the window?*

A. *I fired the other one at the window.*

Q. *Was there anybody in that room where you fired?*

A. *I never seen anybody in there but this shot that hit so low I thought come from the window.*

Q. *Did you see where there was a part of a log knocked out where a shot could come through?*

A *No, Sir, the end of the house where we were, because it wasn't logged.*

.Mr. Chambers, do you have any more questions for this witness? No Sir.

The Powers' attorney James Fielder cross examined Deputy Marshal Haynes, pointing out first that in his testimony that at the northeast corner of our house, about two feet from the house, was the remains of a shake fence about five feet long. Mr. Fielder pointed out that there never was a fence built in Kilburn Canyon while we were there, and if there is one there now, it has been built by someone while we were sleeping and was not visible in either day or night Haynes gave further testimony about the trip to the mine to pick up the Power family;

"for which we had warrants."

There was no mention whatsoever in the trial or the inquest about the posse's stopping at the Bosco place other than Haynes stating that they rode by the Bosco home but did not stop because there was nobody at home.

Attorney Fielder pointed out that Mr. and Mrs. Bosco testified at the inquest that they were both home and up preparing breakfast when they heard the four men ride by their home with Kane Wooten who was in the lead waving as they stepped out the front door to see what was causing the commotion so early that Sunday morning. Sadly. the evidence of perjury on the part of Haynes made no impression on the judge or the jury.

The next and other main witness for the state was none other than Jay Murdock, whose ranch was in between the Bosco place and the Power Garden cabin, questioned by the prosecutor;

Q. What is your name?

A. J.J. Murdock

Q. Where do you live, Mr. Murdock?

A. Up in the Galiuro Mountains.

Q. Do you know where the Powers' mining camp is located?

A. Yes, sir.

Q. How far from that camp is it to where you live?

A. Well, about, a little over half a mile a mile.

Q. I will ask you to state whether or not you were present there Sunday morning.

A. Sir?

Q. Last Sunday morning, were you Present at your place last Sunday morning?

A. Was I?

Q. (Of counsel) Yes.

A. (Of counsel) Yes sir.

Q. Did you hear any shots over in the direction? of the Powers' camp.

A. Yes, sir.

Q. About how many shots did you hear

fired over there?

A It would have been hard to tell just how many, but they were coming so fast, you know, it sounded like rifle shots and six-shooter shots all at the same time, really like a machine gun, just pop, pop, pop, like that, maybe their might have been twenty or twenty-five shots fired.

Q. After that, did you see Tom Sisson, John Power or Tom Power?

A. After that, yes, sir.

Q. Where did you see them?

A. Just about twenty-five yards this side, towards Powers' camp from my house; that would be north.

Q. What were they doing there?

A. They were coming up the trail, on horseback toward my place.

Q. Did you then talk to them?

A. Yes, sir.

Q. All right, now just related the conversation that occurred when you were able to talk with them.

A. Well, sir, I had started out with my horse, and got about twenty-five yards from my house and I met the three of them in the trail, and the first thing I said was, "It has happened?" They said, "you're damned right, it has happened." And I said, "Tell me how it was, and where is your father?" They said, "They shot him and he is wounded.?" I said, "Is he dead?" They said, "No I asked them, who they were and they told me it was Kane Wooten and Frank McBride and Frank's brother. Then they all began talking.

Little Tom Power said that his father stepped out in the yard and that they told him to throw up his hands and he said their father dropped his gun and threw up his hands and Kane Wooten shot their father, when he had his hands in the air. Kane turned around and shot through the window and filled Tom's eye full of glass his left eye was all swollen up-and he said, "I took my rifle and punched out the rest of the window and killed Kane Wooten."

Q. That was Tom Power saying that?

A. Yes, sir.

Q. Did any of the others say anything then, anymore?

A. Yes, John Power says, "well I killed McBride," then, "what's the matter with your face, have you been in a roughhouse?" He said it was splinters His face was bloody and the blood was dried all over his face; it was just as bloody as it could be. He said it was splinters that had a cut his face.

Q. And Sisson claimed that he shot one too, did he?

A. I didn't hear that part. By the time the rest of them had gone down there from the house and was taking questions and all three of them was talking at the same time and I didn't hear that part. I didn't hear anyone say Tom Sisson killed the other man.

Q. When you had this first part of the conversation, you were talking to him alone?

A. By myself. By the time the rest of them got down in there and were all talking, asking questions pretty fast.

Q. Now, you say you made the remark, "It has happened?"

A. Yes, sir.

Q. How did you come to make that remark?

A. Well, sir, they were there and I knew it and I looked for Mack to come after them all the time. Mack had given me a letter when I was here last, about ten or fifteen days ago, to take out to old man Power, and he told me to read the letter. He gave it to me in the sheriff's office here in Safford. He knew in his own mind that the boys were in there and I was looking for Mack to come. I read the letter myself.

Q. Do you know what became of that letter?

A. No, sir. I gave it to old man Power myself.

Q. What was the substance of that letter?

A. That was a fine letter as I ever read. It was a well put up letter. He explained to the boys him and I talked it over and I told him that I didn't believe they realized what it meant to do what they were doing. Mack and I was talking here in the sheriff's office, and he said he would write this letter and explain it to them and show the boys Mack says, "Maybe I can explain and show the boys the mistake that they are making by slacking like they are." They read the letter. I cannot repeat the letter, but it was a fine letter, an awful fine letter, explaining to the

boy's what it really meant to be a
slacker, to be a traitor to their country
and so on and so forth. He said, "It is
not my duty as sheriff to arrest you
boys, the government will take it up
with you both someday, and if you can
get the boys to come in and give up,"
He said, "I think I can get them
through without prosecution and let
them go on to the front and join the
army." Only one time that they ever
referred to this letter to me; the next
time I seen them old man Power says
to me, he says, "Well, McBride says
he isn't coming up."

Q. Did you talk with them about coming
   in?
A. Did I talk to them about coming in?
A. (Of counsel) Yes
A. No, sir.
Q. Had they ever talked to you at all
   about what they were going to do if
   the officers came for them?
A. Yes, sir.
Q. What had they said?
A. I had seen them. I suppose you
   Remember, they had a sister living out
   there, Power's daughter, who died
   a month or so ago. I saw him about
   two or three days after the funeral. I
   went to the house and they were
   there, after dark.
Q. The boys were there?
A. Yes, sir, old man Power, Tom Sisson,
   John Power and Tom Power, all four
   of them. I went over to find out how
   this happened; the girl died and she
   had been buried before I knew it. They

sent a man over for me and I came over to see how this thing happened. They told me that they hauled the body to Klondyke and I knew then that the officers knew no doubt that they were in there and I didn't feel very safe sitting there among these slackers. I made a remark, "Suppose McBride and his posse would walk in here?" Little Tom Power says, "let him come; "I'd just as soon die now as any time and while they're getting me, I'll get some of them, maybe more than they get of us." Therefore, I always felt that at any minute somebody was going to come in there after them.

Q. Now, was that before you took this letter out?

A. Yes, sir. That was maybe three weeks or a month before.

Q. Did you tell McBride about that?

A. Yes, sir, yes, sir. I told his undersheriff too.

Q. Told Kempton about it?

A. Both of them, yes, sir, in the sheriff's office. I talked to Mack an hour about it and then I guess I was another hour and a half talking to Kempton.

Q. At the time you gave the letter to old man Power, did he make any remark?

A. None whatever. I told Mack like this, I said, "Mack, I have got live up there; I don't like to take any sides on either side of this thing, because if they got it in for me they would bump me off just as quick as anybody else."

That's the expression I used to Mack. "Therefore, I don't like to carry anything," I said, He told me then what he was going to write him, you know, explaining to these boys what it really meant to be a slacker. So when he told me that, I said, "All right, Mack, if you are going to write that letter I will carry that letter right there, and when I brought the letter I said that I had been talking to Mack and that Mack told me that he didn't believe that they realized what they were doing and that he was going to write a letter and would I take it out. I went in my inside pocket and pulled out the letter and handed it to him. He took the letter and looked at it and went over and put it on the shelf and a few days after he told me that Mack told them that he wasn't coming.

Q. Did he say anything else about the letter?

A. Sir?

Q. Was that all that was said about the letter?

A. That was the only time that the letter Was every mentioned to me after I gave it to him.

Q. Anything else said any talk about whether or not they would come in?

A. Did they ever say anything more about coming? in and giving up?

Q. (of counsel), Yes.

A. No, Sir.

Q. Did they ever say anything more about What they would do if they came after them?

A. Oh, yes, they told me that they would fight till they died. They told me once that they would kill anybody that came over that trail that looked like they might be in there after them. That's why the night before a cowboy came over to my house, the night before the killing, and stayed all night with me and was going to ride in that country the next day.

Q. Who was that?

A. Red, the cowboy, they called him; his name is Nutal, he works for the Mule Shoe Cattle Company on the other slope of the mountains. He said he had a couple of steers running up there and he came up there to look for these steers and stayed at my house that night. He said he was going to ride over Grassy Peak the next day. They had told me that they would kill anybody that rode that trail, and to keep these boys from probably hurting him, the night before the killing, I saddled up my horse and rode over and told them that Red the cowboy was at my house and that he was going to ride over Grassy Peak, the next day to look for a couple of steers, and I say, "You want to leave him alone for he is not here for you boys." I say, "don't bother that boy, he is not looking for you at all." They didn't seem to like it very well, they said, "All right." I turned around and went back home. I meant next morning to go with him until we passed their place to see him safely by. If he was with me, naturally they would not bother him. He was there when the boys come, after they had killed these men, he was in my yard.

Q. How were they getting their provisions up there, do you know?

A. I think they got them mostly from Safford and Klondyke. They had an automobile down in the canyon, you know. They would go down on horses and then go in the car; that is the way I heard them speak of coming in.

Q. Did you know if they had provisions with them? other side that is?

A. Not that I know of, no sir; I don't think so.

Q. After the killing did you go up to the house?

A. Yes, sir.

Q. What did you find there?

A. I found three dead men and one wounded.

Q. Did you know these dead men?

A. I know two of them to be sure, and the other one was Kempton, I couldn't tell whether he was A.G. Walker or Mr. Kempton. I never knew until the party got there and told me it was Kempton.

Q. You knew McBride and Wooten?

A. I knew Frank McBride and I knew Kane Wooten.

Q. What were the positions the bodies lying when you got up there?

A. Kane Wooten and Mr. Kempton were the first bodies we saw, then we got to Mr. Kempton was lying with his foot towards the east and his head to the west, on his side, and Kane Wooten was lying with his feet to the north and his head to the south, with his head facing downhill, and lying flat on his back. He had his right leg kind of drawn up a little bit and kind of on Mr. Kempton's head.

Q. It was that way when you first saw them?

A. When I first got to them, yes.

Q. Were those bodies disturbed any?

A. A little louder?

Q. Were those bodies disturbed any before the posse got up there that morning?

A. No sir, not anymore. You see after we got Mr. Power carried to the tunnel it was snowing right hard. I said to father, "I am going to go up and cover those bodies up." He said, "You had better leave them alone because the law requires that you should not molest the bodies at all." I said, "I'm not going to move them, I'm just going to get a canvas and spread it over them, for if I spread this canvas over them when they get here they can just lift it up and everything will show just as it is." So I went up and covered the bodies with this canvas. I put a big wagon sheet over them and weighed it down with rocks; then I went over to Mack. His head had fallen in a bush. I put kind of a rug over his head, kind of packed the brush down, and I put kind of old canvass mattress over the rest of his body and covered him up the best I could.

Q. Now, then what did you do with Old Man Power?

A. I left him in the tunnel. I had cut his

clothes off; I had him naked. I had cut his clothes off before he died.

Q. What did you do right at the time when your first went up there?

A. When I first got to the place?

A. (of counsel) Yes.

A. (of counsel) When I first got up there-Henry Allen was the first man to get to him. They told me he was-the boys told me, they said, "You will find the old man in some brush by the arastra, there was two arastras there, one new one and one old one, and they found the old man by the old arastra. I was first hunting there by the new arastra 70 or 80 yards from there. Henry had taken the trail to the left on the other hillside and I went up the trail on the right. Henry found him first. When I got up to him he was unconscious. Father and I got there about the same time. When we straightened him out, he was lying all crooked and his eyes were glassy. I asked him, "Do you know who I am?" This is Jay, do you know who Jay Murdock is?" He didn't know me, father said, "This is Dad." He didn't know either of us. When we got him straightened out Henry and I ran to the house to see whether any of these other people might be wounded, living, but they were dead. I went to get water and went back, and the old man was conscious then. The first thing he said he knew me he said, "Give me a drink of water." I poured water down him.

Q. Did you move the body then?

A. Did I move it then?

A. (of counsel) Yes.

A. Yes, sir.

Q. Where did you take it?

A. Took it down to the tunnel. We carried Him down to the tunnel and put him in The entry tunnel of the mine.

Q. How long did he stay there before he died?

A. Well, he stayed there he didn't die until about four o'clock that evening.

Q. Did you stay there all the time from that time on?

A. All the time.

Q. And hadn't left there from that time on?

A. Had What?

Q. You hadn't left there from that time up to the time the posse arrived there Monday morning?

A. No sir. Oh yes. I knew some of the boys had been there all the time. I went after water.

Q. Did you stay there all night?

A. Yes, sir.

Q. How many of you stayed there all night?

A. Three.

Q. Who were they?

A. My father, myself and Ed Knothe.

Q. Who is this other man?

A. He is a German fellow, a little prospector. He lives about a couple of hundred yards from my house.

Q. Did he go up with you when you first went up there?

A. He was afoot and we were on horseback, and while we were saddling up we told him to go on afoot and we afterwards overtook him, we were running our horses and had our horses on a dead run and passed him up and beat him there.

Q. "Knocthe," Is that the way you pronounce it?

A. "Knothe" he spells it.

Q. Had he been talking to these boys About staying out of the army?

A. About what?

Q. About keeping out of the army, do you know?

A. No, I don't think so. No, he doesn't talk very much. Of course, he talks about the war sometimes.

Q. Never heard him give any expression about these boys going into the army, did you"

A. No, Sir. No, he told me that he thought they we're making a big mistake though.

Q. He did tell you that?

A. Yes, sir.

Q. Now, did you have any conversation with the old man, Power, before he died, about the shooting?

A. About what?

A. (of counsel) about the shooting?

A. (of witness) No sir, he told me that he never knew anything after Kane Wooten shot him until we found him over there on the hill in front of the cabin.

Q. How far was he from the house, where you found him?

A. About sixty-five yards. I guess. Sixty or Sixty-five, somewhere about that.

Q. Whereabouts was he shot?

A. He was shot right about there (indicating upper left breast). The bullet came out right between the shoulder blades.

Q. Could you tell the difference from where the bullet went in and came out?

A. Yes, sir, it was a larger hole in the back than it was in front. He breathed through this bullet hole. He took my fingers and was trying to make a passage once and I raised him up to make it and the wind just fairly whistled through there and I took my fingers and held my fingers over the bullet hole, and he could rest easier that way and breathe better.

Q. When you closed it up, you mean?

A. Yes, he could breathe easier. The wind just whistled through there and it bled awful bad.

Q. What did he say about what happened before he was shot?

A. He said he didn't know there was anybody around. He said, "I stepped out in the yard, they hailed me and hollered 'throw up your hands?' and I dropped my gun and throwed up my hands and I says, 'We give up!' and then Kane Wooten shot me."

Q. That was what he said?

A. He repeatedly told me that all day.

Q. Did he say that was the first shot that was fired?

A. Yes, he said that was the first shot.

Q. Was there anything else that he said that had anything to do with regard to the shooting?

A. Only that he would say, "I don't know what they wanted to shoot me for. I had my hand up begging them for peace.

Q. Did he seem to think he was going to die?

A. Yes, sir. I encouraged him all the time. He kept on saying, "Jay, I am going to die, I can't stand it." I would say, "No, Mr. Power, you are as good as a dozen dead men yet, and are shot too high to die, you will get on all right just as quick as we get a doctor here." I kept telling him that up to he died.

Mr. Chambers:

I think that is all the questions I have.

Juror: Q

. How long did the shooting last?

A. About three minutes.

Q. Three minutes. Was there any shots fired after that?

A. After that?

A. (Of Juror) Yes, after the main shooting occurred?

A. (Of witness) It was like a machine gun going there while it lasted, just as fast as it could go, and it sounded like big guns and little guns all together, and then it stopped right suddenly. There was a space maybe of half a minute or more. Then bang went one rifle, "pop, pop, pop" went an automatic six-shooter five or six shots just as rapidly as anyone could pull a trigger.

Q. After that there was no more shooting?

A. That was the last I heard.

Q. Did you notice around Frank's head?

was there anything to Indicate that he received a shot in the head after he had fallen?

A. No, sir. You see, the way I felt about Frank. I look at those other two men just the same as I could look at any dead man, but when I went around to look at Frank he had one eye closed and the other eye open looking right straight at me. I looked at him for a second and I could see he was just as white as could be and I knew he was dead. I could see a great big blood spot down here on his side. I turned around then and walked away; it kind of got on my nerves a little bit, that eye looking like that then when I come to cover him up. I looked at him again, then I put this rug thing over his face and put the mattress on him, then of course, I couldn't see him no more.

A juror questions the witness

Q. About what time did you get to the camp?

A. About 8:30 o'clock, I guess.

Q. You got up to there camp about 8:30 o'clock?

A. I guess about, I didn't have any watch nor kept any time, just guessed at the time. I think just about a half an hour or so before, I mean after the shooting, we got there, because I'll tell you. I had just got out of bed and put my clothes on and was building a fire in the stove when this battle opened up. Then I jumped in and got breakfast and just started to go down to the get the horses and then we ran the horses all the way up there.

Mr. Chambers takes the stand.

Q. What time do you think it was, when the Power boys and Sisson passed your camp?

A. It must have been about, oh, maybe about eight o'clock or a quarter past eight.

Q. Then it wasn't over half or three-quarters of an hour after the Shooting?

A. It couldn't have been more than half or three- quarters of an hour, I don't think.

Mr. Chambers:

All right, that is all. the court, Any more questions? That's all.

Mr. Fielder, our attorney cross examined Mr. Murdock right after his testimony. His first line of questioning was to point out to the jury that Murdock testified that he heard our father say over and over until he died;

"Why did Kane Wooten shoot me, when I had my hands up, and was yelling, that we give up and we did not want to fight."

The second line of questioning of Murdock was to show that he had a tendency to over exaggerate or outright lie. We never met him on the trail from our cabin to his place. He stepped out of the door of his cabin as we rode by and we waved to him and we shouted that it had happened and we asked him to go up to our cabin and take care of our father. We told him as we rode by that he was dead and that he would also find the bodies of three officers lying dead in the yard. He told us that he heard the shooting and that he and his son along with another neighbor Henry Allen would go up to our place and take care of our father and the other men that were in the shootout. Murdock answered all of our attorney's questions and said that he could have been mistaken regarding his testimony that we admitted to him that we had killed the officers. There was no way that he could see any side arms we were carrying as we had on our overcoats.

Regarding the testimony of the letter that was suppose to have been delivered to us. We never saw any letter nor did we ever see any letter from Sheriff McBride. The letter was never produced in court and if it did exist it would have been found by the posse that went up to their cabin and ransacked the cabin and all of the other Power buildings.

Attorney Fielder also pointed out that the first we heard about the slacker accusation was when the soldiers picked them up in Mexico. Lieutenant Hayes testified that he was surprised when we told him we would not shoot a soldier. He then knew we could have killed him and all of his patrol before they saw us, but we put up our hands and surrendered without a fight

Attorney Fielder tried to subpoena the postmaster at Redington so that he could testify that the boys had come in and attempted to register and that he sent them home and told them that if the government needed them that he would send a forest service ranger to get them. He also pointed out that Sheriff McBride had no legal right to arrest anyone for being slackers. Failing to report for the draft was a U.S. Government law and not a state law. Sadly, the postmaster had joined the army and was stationed in France when the trial took place and they were not able to get his testimony. Fielder did present evidence indicating that even if they had registered that the Arizona State lottery for the draft that it was closed because our allotment had already been reached. This was exactly what the postmaster at Redington told them when they went to register for the draft. Not being able to subpoena the postmaster left us in a position that we were not able to prove that we went Redington to register.

Their attorney also questioned Murdock regarding the cowboy that he met. He testified that "*Red the cowboy, his name is Nuttall,*" and stayed at Murdock's tent the night before the shooting, and was going to Grassy Peak the next day. Murdock said he rode over to tell them about the cowboy the night before the shooting, because they had threatened to kill anybody that rode the trail. First of all, there was no one named Nuttall in that area. The cowboy he referred to was Sol Ray. Murdock did not ride over to their house the Saturday night before the shooting. In fact, Sol Ray stopped by their cabin the night before the shooting and ate dinner with the Power family. He told them when he left that he was going on down and spend the night at his friend Jay Murdock's place.

Mr. Fielder also brought up the fact Murdock testified that the Power brothers went to Safford quite regularly and to Klondyke regularly for provisions. This would show that if the officers were really serious about being after them, they could have picked up the boys at any time they were in either town and there was no need to ambush the Power family and Tom Sisson at daybreak on Sunday February 10th 1918.

The County Attorney Mr. Chambers recognized that this was a weak point in the case he was putting together. He was trying to lead Murdock to say we were holed up at our place and an old cave farther up in Heilberg Canyon.

In fact, we had used the old cave several years before to live while we worked three more mine claims we owned because the claims were five miles from our cabin. We simply left some old can goods there along with two cots plus some mining equipment we used to work the claim.

As mentioned above, Jay Murdock and his father John were used by the state to defame the Power's characters. Jay Murdock testified that the brothers were always making threats, and that they packed guns. Every man or woman in that area packed guns at that time. He said they threatened to shoot anybody who came up our trail. And yet people were passing both of our cabins going back and forth on a regular basis without our family ever raising a hand. In fact, we were always being congenial and helpful. Far from the testimony that was given by both Jay and his father John Murdock.

In fact, after John (not JJ, his son) Murdock took the stand and testified as a state character witness, Mr. Fielder was allowed to cross examine him. He started the questioning by asking John;

> *"What about your own character?*
> *What do you think it's worth?"*

John looked around the courtroom and said out loud;

> *"I think it's as good as any man's*
> *here."*

When he was finished talking, Mr. Fielder said;

> *"Oh, I don't think so,"*

Mr. fielder replied,

> *"I think, in fact, I know, there are*
> *not many people here who have been*
> *tried and convicted of a high crime*
> *such as rape and sentenced from 30*
> *years to life at the prison in Yuma,*
> *Arizona."*

Old man Murdock slumped down in his chair saying out loud enough for all to hear;

> *"Yea, but I never got there. They*
> *got together and pulled me off the*

train. I understand that is what happened,'

Mr. Fielder and he did not question the elder Murdock any further at that time but he did say as Murdock was released;

"I think I am going to have the Attorney General look into the case to see what actually happened and why you got out of serving the prison term."

The last witness to testify at the trial was Doctor W.E. Platt who was the physician that performed the autopsy on the bodies of the three fallen officers, Frank McBride, Mart Kempton and Kane Wooten. There was no autopsy performed on Old Man Power. Platt was sworn in and the County Prosecutor Mr. Chambers did the questioning.

Q. What is your name?
A. W. E. Platt
Q. What is your business?
A. Physician and surgeon
Q. Doctor, I will ask you to state whether or not you had occasion to examine the bodies of the three dead officers on evening of February 10th 1918.
A. Yes, sir.
Q. Whose bodies were they?
A. Frank McBride, Mart Kempton and Kane Wooten.
Q. Now, I will ask you first to take McBride's Body and state what you found.
A. Frank McBride was shot in the knee, the right knee, at about this point (indicating); a small entrance hole and a very large just about an inch and a half, right through the joint of the knee and it came out a big tear in the inner surface. And two balls through the body; the upper ball just in the last rib here, it entered,

and came out about an inch higher than it went in on the opposite side. This ball was lying next to the skin. The shot below was two and one half inches below the upper one and the ball didn't quite go through; you could feel the ball on the other surface. A ball entered the right side of the head and passed out the left; entered on the right side of the ear here and came out on the same angle, same level, on the opposite side of the neck.

Q. How many of those shots would have Produced death.

A. Three.

Q. Were those shots down here in the stomach, would those have Produced immediate death?

A. No, sir. He was probably living until he received
this shot in the head.

Q. The Court: (Producing the remains of the bullet) What's that, Doctor, did you find that in the body?

A. Yes, sir. That was in the upper wound near The point of exit.

Q. Mr. Chambers: His head, do you mean?

A. No, sir; on the chest, the abdomen.

Q. Now in reference to Kempton, what did you observe as to bullet wounds.

A. Kempton received only one shot. It entered exactly in the center of the neck and carried away the first, second and third vertebrae.

Q. In the back?

A. In the back, and came out at the side of the jaw and just tore the whole side of the jaw out. That is the only injury he received.

Q. You didn't find the bullet?

A. No, sir. No, it was a soft bullet and went clear through.

Q. That is a wound that would have produced instant death?

A. Instant death, yes, sir. He bled to death inside of three minutes, I would say.

Q. In your opinion did that bullet go in at the back or the front?

A. It passed in from the back and came out at The front. It tore the whole ear away and nearly all of the jaw to here.

Q. Now, how many bullet wounds did you find on Wooten?

A. One.

Q. Where was that?

A. The ball entered to the right of the median line, or to the left of the median line in the third vertebra and passed forward and a little bit upward and exited an inch and a half from the sternum, the center of the chest, and tore out a hole as big as three silver dollars.

Q. Was the hole bigger in front than it was behind?

A. Yes, sir, the point of entrance was a very small hole and the other was a very large one.

Q. In your opinion then Wooten was shot from the back and not from the front?

A. Yes, sir, Wooten was shot from the back.

Q. Was that a hole such as would produce instant death?

A. Instant death, yes, sir. He also had a bruise on his face that looked like heel of a boot.

Q. Didn't notice anything like that on McBride?

A. No, I didn't notice any. Kane Wooten had another mark on the left hand about this position (indicating), which showed the heel injury, and then the rest of the body was scarred in two or three places; I don't know whether that was produced before or after death. The one looked like it was produced before death and the other one looked like it might have after his death. Mr. Chambers: That's all, I guess, The Court: That's all Doctor Platt.

After Doctor Platt's testimony Mr. Fielder our attorney cross examined the doctor and pointed to him by asking him if McBride was shot in the lower abdomen with a .41 caliber bullet? The doctor said yes. Then he asked the doctor if the shot that went through McBride's knee was made with a .30 caliber bullet. This shot entered the body from the right and went out through the left. The doctor answered, yes. He went on to ask the doctor if that shot went into McBride from the right side through the body and exited on the left side of the body. The doctor answered yes. He further asked the doctor if that bullet was a .30 caliber and the doctor again answered yes.

Mr. Fielder pointed out to the jury that neither Tom or John Power nor Tom Sisson owned a .30 caliber rifle or pistol. Old man Jeff Power had a .30 caliber Winchester lever action rifle but Deputy Marshal Haynes previously testified that he saw the rifle lying on the ground next to Old Man Power as he lay on the ground about ten feet in front of the cabin door. Mr. Fielder pointed out the fact that only Deputy Marshal Haynes carried a .30 caliber rifle. The other three officers carried .45 or .44 caliber pistols and the Power men owned only rifles.

Mr. Fielder said the facts indicate that Sheriff McBride and his Deputy Kane Wooten were both shot by one or two of their own posse members and the only one that had a .30 caliber rifle was Deputy Marshal Haynes. He further pointed out that Jay Murdock testified that he did not hear any other shots after the gunfight. He pointed out again the fact that since there was no single shot from a pistol that ended Sheriff McBride's life that the shot was made during the gunfight. And since the only officer with a .30 caliber rifle was Haynes; he must have killed Sheriff McBride during the shootout.

Mr. Fielder called John Power as his first witness for the defense and he made a very favorable impression on the jury until asked about his friend Tom Sisson. His testimony came across as an obvious attempt to absolve Sisson of any blame in connection with the deaths. He testified that;

> *"Mr. Sisson was in bed when the shooting started and stayed there all the time it was going on."*

Generally conceded by those attending the trial, this was a bad mistake on John's part, there being a feeling that John fabricated this statement to try to clear Mr. Sisson but it destroyed much of whatever confidence he had gained up to that time. Too much proof existed of the guilt of Big Tom Sisson. If John would lie about this, he would lie about all of it, reasoned the public and eventually the jury.

Tom Power was said to be very disappointed that he did not have the opportunity to testify on his own behalf. To those who understood courtroom testimony, question and answer procedure, the reason Mr. Fielder did not call him was apparent. Because of the spectacle John made of himself during the cross examination, the defense attorney did not dare put Tom on the stand.

Mr. Fielder concluded our defense by pointing out that a man's dying statement had been used as evidence in trials in the past and that Jeff Power's dying statement to Murdock over and over again;

> *"Why did Kane Wooten shoot me when I had my hands in the air."*

This dying man's statement to J.J. Murdock, the son of John Murdock, should be taken into account.

But of course the judge simply shrugged his shoulders and shook his head, and the jury all nodded in compliance.

The jury's time of deliberation was one of the shortest in the history of murder trials, especially with three men accused. In thirty-five minutes they returned with the verdict; guilty of murder in the first degree on all three the defendants. Before passing sentence on the three convicted men they were told to stand before Judge Lain and asked if they had anything to say in their behalf. The Power brothers shook their heads indicating no. Tom Sisson said quite out loud;

"I am not guilty of any crimes!"

The judge said;

"In view of the fact that the jury has found you guilty of murder in the first degree and secondly I have no dissension in the matter, you all will be confined and imprisoned in the state prison in Florence, Arizona or wherever the same may hereafter be located in the State of Arizona, for a period of your natural life. You are remanded to the custody of the Sheriff of the County of Greenlee, State of Arizona, to be by him delivered into the custody of the proper officer of said prison at Florence, Arizona;"

Done in open court, this 20th day of May, 1918; Judge Frank B. Laine, Judge of said Court.

Sadly, James Fielder, their defense attorney, in his closing statement, did not stress two of the most important facts in representing the Power brothers and Tom Sisson. First he did not address the fact that

Dr. W.E. Platt, who performed the autopsy, testified that Sheriff McBride sustained four bullet wounds in the shootout. Two shots came from 45-40 caliber rifles and the two that ended his life came from a .30 caliber rifle, one that hit his knee and the other to his head. The Power boys and Tom Sisson all had rifles. The only .30 caliber gun owned by the Power family was the Winchester lever action rifle of Jeff Power, that lay on the ground next to his body in front of the cabin door. Deputy Haynes testified that Jeff's rifle was lying next to his body as he lay dying in front of the cabin door, so there was no way that he could have shot and killed McBride, and again, the only other person at the gunfight, who shot a .30 Caliber pistol was Deputy Marshall Frank Haynes.

The second fact which was in the testimony of witness Murdock was that during the shootout he heard big guns and little guns being fired. Then all was silent. There was not one more shot that supposedly ended Sheriff McBride's life. Another fact that should have been mentioned was that even if McBride had been shot while lying on the ground with a .30 caliber rifle, the Power boys would have had to take it from one of the three fallen officers and not one of them had such a weapon. This fact goes along with Deputy Marshal Haynes testimony that he and Sheriff McBride fired their pistols into the window and the door of the Power Cabin. In fact, only Deputy Marshal Haynes carried a .30 caliber lever action rifle.

This author submits that the evidence points to the fact that Deputy Marshal Haynes fired the two shots that immediately ended the life of Sheriff. The author has spoken to many police officers who have told him that in a gunfight sometimes the good guys do die. I have no doubt that Deputy Marshal Haynes shot at a body moving in the dark before he realized it was one of his own posse members.

The guilty verdict was mostly based Murdock's testimony that the Power family had threatened to kill anyone who came near their camp. It was used to bring in the first degree murder verdict, which could only have been given if the crime was premeditated. Mr. Fielder proved Murdock's statement was not true as people came by their place on a regular basis, most of them stopping to water their stock or just simply visit with the family, there was also during the trial any mention of the fact that the officers called out to Mr. Power that they had warrants for the arrest of Tom and John for being slackers.

Mr. Fielder told Tom and John that he knew we did not get a fair trial and the national news media was no place in the State of Arizona, that would have helped us to have gotten a fair trial. He told us even though the state would pay the expenses incurred for an appeal with the evidence presented, the biased witnesses, and his rebuttal of all the facts it was not worth it to appeal the decision.

One has to wonder what was going on in Attorney Fielder's head when he made his decision not to appeal the court's decision. This author, based on the research, believes neither County Attorney Chambers nor any of his team proved beyond a doubt that the shootings were premeditated. Even given the mistakes and biased testimony, and the fact that the officers did not announce they had warrants for Tom & John for draft dodgers, which by the way carried a six-week sentence if convicted. Of course we will never know who shot first. According to Haynes testimony, he said the man in the door fired first but Jeff Power, over and over until he died kept saying,

> *"Why did Kane Wooten shoot me*
> *with my hands were in the air."*

A verdict of manslaughter on each defendant should have been the verdict, but when law officers lose their lives in the line of duty, it is a whole different story.

Below is a newspaper article about the verdict that was published in the Tucson Daily Star on May 21st 1918;

GUILTY OF First Degree MURDER

Quick Verdict of Jury in the Power-Sisson Case at Clifton

JURY OUT ONLY 25 MINUTES

John and Tom Power and Tom Sisson Will Get Life Imprisonment

The trial of John and Tom Power and Tom Sisson, charged with the murder of Sheriff R.F. McBride, and his deputies, Martin Kempton and Kane Wooten, on Sunday, February 10th at the home of the Power boys in the Galiuro Mountains, began Monday, at Clifton, in the Superior Court of Greenlee County, Judge Frank Laine, presiding.

A jury was secured by Monday night and the testimony of witnesses for the prosecution began Tuesday morning, closing at 2:00 PM, and followed by the witnesses for the defense.

All the testimony in the case was finished by at 3:00 o'clock yesterday afternoon. Graham County Attorney Chambers gave the closing address before the jury at 2 P.M. And was followed by the closing address from Attorney Fielder for the defense.

Attorney Fielder had not finished his address when court adjourned at 5:00 o'clock, and continued his argument to the jury when court convened this morning, finishing at 11:00 o'clock.

Attorney Johnson, one of the lawyers on the prosecution team made the closing address. Court adjourned at noon for lunch and convened again at 1:30 PM, when Judge Laine delivered his charge to the jury. The jury was given the case at 2:55 o'clock and returned at 3:20 with a verdict of guilty of murder in the first degree for all
three defendants.

The attorneys for the prosecution were County Attorney W.R. Chambers, A.R. Lynch, of Clifton, and Norman Johnson, of Globe. The attorney for the defense was James Fielder, of Silver City, New Mexico.

Chapter Thirteen

After sentencing the men, they were taken to the city jail in Clifton and bound over to the local officials until they could be transported to the new Arizona State Prison in Florence.

On May 21st 1918, Sheriff's Brig Stewart, Arthur Slaughter and Ernest Lancaster came into the jail at one o'clock in the morning. They told us they had decided we should be taken out of the city jail and transported to Florence by automobile. I was convinced there was a lynch mob waiting outside. The sentiment of the town's people was that life imprisonment was not enough punishment.

On the toilets in the jail the flush bars were made of marble and fastened with a simple cotter pin; I grabbed a flush bar and told the officers they would have to kill us right there as we knew we would not be safe with them on any automobile trip to Florence. We told them we would not even make it out of Clifton alive.

Lucky for the boys Sheriff Mack McCarthy, a friend who came with the other officers to pick them up in Lordsburg, New Mexico walked into the jail right at that moment. He stopped the transfer telling the officers the court had ordered the prisoners to be transported by train to Florence. Mack had ridden all the way from New Mexico to Safford and then from Safford to Clifton with them and he never wore a gun. He along with his wife brought us a change of clothes and food. I knew we could trust him.

At daylight that morning we were taken from the jail to the train station. We were handcuffed and shackled together and Sheriff's Stewart, Lancaster and Mack McCarthy accompanied us. We had to change trains in Lordsburg, New Mexico, and offered sandwiches for lunch. We had many friends there; one was a deputy sheriff who brought them good meals and cigarettes.

Tom goes on to say that he remembered after eating lunch we were handcuffed and shackled. The officers wanted to put us in a Pullman car for the trip to Phoenix. However, the conductor would not allow it because we all smoked and he demanded we be put in the smoker car. He told the officers to take off our irons, because there is no way to escape a moving train going 45 mph. Our handcuffs were removed but they left on the shackles. On the trip Sheriff Stewart asked me;

> *"What are you going to learn while you're there in prison?"*

Tom told him that he was going to study law. The sheriff told Tom they would probably not be there more than eight or nine months and if it stretched longer than eighteen months he would recommend us for parole. During the train ride to Phoenix Sheriff Stewart told John and I that we had been given a raw deal. Tom went on to say that after ten years of our being incarcerated, that Stewart actually did send a recommendation to the parole board at the State Prison in Florence that we be paroled.

The train arrived in Phoenix at dusk on the 21st of May. The officers had us ride in taxicabs to the jail; on the way we stopped at a small restaurant for supper. We spent the night in the Phoenix jail; the next morning we were taken to Florence, about 60 miles south east of Phoenix. Riley Brian, captain of the guards at the Florence State Prison, met us at the gate and had his officers remove our shackles and handcuffs. We were taken to the Yard Office for a shakedown and a picture was taken before we were led to the barbershop for head shavings and shaves. Next stop was the bathhouse where our bodies were examined for scars and any identifying marks. After bathing we were to get clean clothes but they had none available in our size. Our old clothes were returned. These were the same clothes Mack and his wife had given us in Clifton. We wore them for seven months until they wore out; only then did we receive our prison clothes.

After our bath, they took us back to the picture studio for our prison picture portraying us with bald heads. John and I were assigned to cell 22 in the Number 1 Cell House, but we were not sure what cell was assigned to Mr. Sisson.

Our prison sentence started that day and we soon learned the prison procedures. The first wake-up whistle sounded at 7 o'clock the next morning. The next whistle was about a half hour later for the head count. Men who slept in the yard were first to be counted. Next the remaining prisoners were released from their cell blocks and dormitories. Two whistles were blown for breakfast.

At 8 o'clock every morning the work whistle signals for us to meet at the front gate to be assigned our work duty for the day. John, Tom and Mr. Sisson were instructed to go to the Yard office to be assigned jobs. Tom said they were sent to the shower room and recreation hall with buckets of soap and water. Their job was to scrub and mop both rooms until dry. Tom said the three of them worked with a lifer named Louis Victor Eiting who showed them what was to be expected of them.

Tom said that breakfast in prison usually consisted of some type of cereal such as oatmeal but no milk or sugar, just water and no coffee or bread. At noon there was a lunch whistle. Lunch usually consisted of beef stew. The supper whistle sounded around 5 o'clock in the evening and dinner was usually beans or beans and rice. At around 6 o'clock in the evening they were locked up for the night. Tom said they were allowed to check out books from the prison library and they were allowed to read until it got dark. Tom read all of the law books but after reading them he realized how all of their rights were violated during their trial and he got so mad he threw the books in the corner and never looked at them again.

When we first got to the prison, there was one guard on each wall for each shift, 12 in all. Later two guards were taken off the front wall during the day shifts, and only one guard was on each wall at night. They walked around the cell blocks watching to make sure there was no crazy stuff happening during the nights.

The prison had a very limited budget when we first arrived. There were no clothes furnished to the prisoners. The food was enough most of the time-although the prison sometimes ran out, but it was all very plain. The only things we always had in plenty of were coffee and bread. There was no garden except at the warden's house.

There were no lights in the cell blocks until Tom fixed the equipment in the power house. The guards used flashlights at night. At first there were no radios, but once the power was fixed the men could keep radios in their cells and men were allowed to read until 10 o'clock when the lights and power to the cell blocks were turned off.

The prisoners worked all week and half a day Saturday unless they were trustees, or held the kind of jobs that had to be done daily. A prisoner had to buy a newspaper if he wanted one to read. After John and Tom made a little money they subscribed to the Arizona Republic for many years. We would share our papers with the other inmates after we read them.

The prison had a tremendous library and a prisoner could check out books any free time which was mostly Saturday afternoons and all day Sundays. There was a recreation hall, but it had nothing in it but a couple of tables where the men could play checkers or dominoes. The men gambled at those tables.

There was not much to do on the weekends. The men just lay around the yard. On Sundays, once in a great while, we would get some special foods; years later the prison had boxing, baseball, and basketball teams for each cellblock and they had tournaments among the prisoners.

On the second day of their new life in prison, Tom said he and John were put to scraping the paper roofing off the top of the office building. They worked at that job for a few days. Then John got sick and had to go into the infirmary and Tom said he was assigned to the power house. The prison had its own electrical system, but both of the boilers were down, and both engines were broken. Smudge pots were being used on the walls for lights.

John had a temperature of 107 degrees and was placed in a bathtub of ice. The doctor there also treated his eyes. He removed some more of the splinters that had been there all this time. John was in the prison hospital about 15 days and the diagnosis was that he had some type of crazy infection the doctor said probably came from an infection in his eye that traveled through his body. When he was released both of his eyes healed enough that he was no longer bothered with them. He had sight in his right eye, but he was totally blind in his left eye.

As soon as Tom and John were settled in prison, Tom began to write letters to try to get a copy of the transcript of their trial, as well as letters to friends asking them to get transcripts for them. In prison we were simply told there was no transcript. The transcript, if there was one, should have been sent to prison with them, and should have been available to be reviewed by the Pardon and Parole Board, and by the Governor of the State of Arizona. In fact, the trial record by the court recorder was never transcribed.

However, it took 34 years for Tom to find out this very discouraging fact. It was rather obvious that the trial was not transcribed for a reason. There were so many important facts neglected during the trial. There was clear evidence that should have put doubt in the jurors' minds, yet the folks in and around Safford and Clifton just didn't want any record of the trial. It remains a travesty of justice. The key question remains. Why?

The Arizona Legislature passed a sheaf of bills as a result of the shooting in addition to the false publicity that surrounded it. Arizona State Senate Bill No.18; passed on June 15th 1918, decreed that it should be unlawful for any person, firm or corporation to give aid, comfort or employment to a slacker. The bill also outlined the punishment for each violation of this law.

A law was also passed by the State Senate and House of Representatives to reinstate the death penalty. This law was a result of the Powers-Sisson murder conviction for killing three officers. There was no doubt that Judge Lain was very discouraged when he had to pass a sentence of life imprisonment. Hanging the three of them was definitely foremost in the judge's mind, that fact was obvious by his demeanor when he issued the judgment.

Arizona State House Bill No. 9 was passed on June, 17th 1918. This law was called Relief of Widows of Slain Officers.

HB 9 allowed the dead officers' widows to file separate wrongful death claims, which were filed by their Attorney R.L Sprigs. The following is a breakdown of each judgment by the Superior Court of Arizona on October 15th 1918: Clara McBride the widow of Sheriff Frank McBride was awarded $30,000; Laura Wooten the widow of Deputy Kane Wooten was awarded $30,010; and Sena Kempton the widow of Mart Kempton was awarded $20,000. A byproduct of House Bill No. 9 was that $17,500 was appropriated out of the State's General Fund to be distributed as follows: McBride's widow got $7,500; Kane Wooten's wife and Mart Kempton's wife each received $5,000. The money was to go to each widow when their children came of age; if the widows died before that, the money was to be divided among their children

To satisfy these judgments the court liquidated all of the mine claims owned by the power family in the Rattlesnake Mining District along with all of the tools, equipment and personal belongings of the Power family and Tom Sisson. A sheriff's sale was held on August the 4th 1918 the funds were split three ways by the widows. The following was the breakdown:

One bay horse-sold to J.W. Allen---------- --$26.00
A bay horse sold to Ed Richardson------ - $13.00
A sorrel horse sold to Alma Peterson---- --$22.00
A dun horse sold to J.B. Weathersby -   -$50.00
A dun horse sold to George Peck- ----- -- -$31.00
A bay mare sold to N. Skaggs-   ----------- --$33.50
A sorrel horse sold to Ed Richard- ---------$15.50
A Brown mare sold to N. Skagg----- ------ -$23.50
A red cow sold to J.I. Massey for --- --------$25.00
A riding saddle sold to J.F. Wooten-   ------$ 6.00
A riding saddle sold to Alma Peterson- ----$ 8.50
A riding saddle sold to Emert Kempton-- --$ 3.50
One pair of silver spurs sold to S. Fletcher.$ 6.50
One 405 caliber rifle sold to H. Bryce--------$10.00
A 35 caliber rifle sold to George Jacobson-$16.00
A 45 caliber pistol sold to Vic Holding- - ---$ 4.00
A 38 caliber pistol sold to Christensen-- - -$11.00
A telescope sold to A.H. Austin-------- ------$ 7.50
A guitar sold to F. Lard--------- ----------- ---$ 7.50
A Ford touring car sold to H. Skaggs --- -$305.00
There was a list of tools, mining equipment
and other personal belongings sold to
Clara McBride-----------------------------------$250.00
A total of all the belongings that were
Sold at the sheriff's sale and split three

Ways among the three widows of the
slain officers totaled -------------- --------- -$906.00

Another result of the wrongful death claims filed by the three widows was the dispersing of the seven mining claims in the Rattlesnake Mining District owned by the Power family. The claims were auctioned by Notice of a Sheriff's Sale, at 2:00 PM, on the steps of the courthouse in Safford, Arizona on November 15, 1918. The sale was issued by Sheriff B.F. Stewart. It was hoped the sale results would cover the $80,010 in judgments that had been awarded to the three widows of the slain officers.

According to Wendy, in the Graham County Assessor's office, Clara McBride was the highest bidder at the sheriff's sale and she was awarded all of the mining claims owned by the Power family for $2,500. The list of the claims that were auctioned on 11/15/1918 are noted here;

> *Abandon No. One, amended location of which is recorded in Book 18, Records of Mines of Graham County, AZ, at page 228*
>
> *Abandon No. Two, amended location of which is recorded in Book 18, Records of Mines of Graham County, AZ, at page 229*
>
> *Abandon No. Three, amended location of which is recorded in Book 18, Records of Mines of Graham County, AZ, at page 230*
>
> *Abandon No. Four, amended location of which is recorded in Book 16, Records of Mines of Graham County, AZ, at page 98*
>
> *Gold Leaf No, one, amended location of which is recorded in Book 23, Records of Mines of Graham County, AZ, at page 49*
>
> *Lee No. One and Lee No. two.*

All seven of the above mining claims are located in the Rattlesnake Mining District, Graham County, in the State of AZ.

The author found according to Nyle Niemuth of the Arizona Mining Museum and Archives, the ore total taken out of the Rattlesnake Mining District from 1923 to 1940 was 100 ounces of Gold and 1,400 ounces of silver. The value of the gold at that time was $20.35 per ounce or a total of $2,035.00 in gold ore and silver at that time was $.65 per ounce or a total value of silver ore was $910.00. The total value of gold and silver mined over the seventeen years was $2,945.00. Nyle further told me that according to the Arizona State Mining records, the Rattlesnake Mining District which included the Power Gold Leaf Mine was only worked from 1923 to 1925 and these were the only records to be found.

Several newspaper articles published mid October of 1933 indicated ore was being taken out of the Gold Leaf Mine, and shipped by wagon to Safford. The ore was sent to El Paso for processing. Arizona has no records as to the amount taken from the mine or the value.

Shortly after the boys' imprisonment, John wrote to Judge Frank B. Lain and asked him to recommend the three of us for parole. John based his request on the fact that their Defense Attorney Fielder always smelled of alcohol during the trial. John said he felt we were not represented correctly based on the fact that our attorney was under the influence of alcohol.

The judge wrote us back a very pointed letter, indicating that he knew attorney Fielder seemed to be under the influence of alcohol during the trial, and was incapable of a proper defense, but he would not advise a recommendation for our parole.

The question one has to ask is, if the judge knew their attorney was not capable of defending the Power brothers and Tom Sisson why didn't he rule a mistrial? Apparently the sentiment ran so high because of the deaths of the three officers a murder conviction would have been eminent, even if there was a mistrial. At this point the brothers knew that it didn't matter who had represented them or if they were given a new trial that a guilty verdict was for sure going to be the outcome. They were just thankful that the state of Arizona had repealed the death penalty as an enticement to gain statehood.

Over the years Deputy Marshal Haynes was a frequent visitor of Tom Power, while the boys were in prison. Haynes was the only surviving officer of the shootout at their cabin. Tom knew Haynes very well, having bootlegged whiskey under his protection. Haynes even talked to the warden about getting a pardon for them. It was obvious even though he never divulged any information about the gunfight, he wanted our forgiveness. We believed he had a guilty conscience, and was relieved when we told him we carried no grudge against him. We told him we were glad he had gotten away or he too, would have been killed. Haynes passed away sometime in the 1930's taking the truth with him.

Chapter Fourteen

For the whole time that Tom and John Power were in prison they continued with their efforts to gain their release. Their willingness to work hard along with their experienced knowledge of so many prison procedures made them highly regarded. They were sought after by several departments in the prison and in most cases were put in charge of many different work projects.

One afternoon after the warden and his staff finished their lunch, Tom approached the warden with an idea he had to save money on the food budget and create a surplus. He said that got the attention of the warden who listened intently to his idea. Tom pointed out if they had their own farm and raised their own cattle, chickens and hogs to feed the prisoners they would have good food and could cut their food budget by maybe two thirds. Tom and John were tired of the prison food and they felt that by dangling a carrot in front of the warden they could, *"kill two birds with one stone."* The prison would have extra income, the guards and prisoners would be able to eat fresher, better food, and it would make the warden look good.

The warden immediately put Tom and John in charge of clearing the land to prepare it for a prison ranch. Tom formed two teams of 40 men each to clear the land by removing all the trees, shrubs, and large rocks. Tom instructed both teams to dig down two feet to remove the rocks and be sure to uncover all the roots from the trees and shrubs. This would allow space for good topsoil. Tom was in charge of team one and John was in charge of team two. Each team was accompanied by three guards. The teams were able to use a large Army truck the prison owned to transport the men from the prison to the future ranch. They used the truck to move large boulders, trees, pull stumps and haul debris to a dumping site.

Tom said it took them about three months to clear five acres of rough desert land. The warden sent several tons of topsoil and mulch that was used to enhance the soil. Sometime in February they finished clearing the land, readying the soil for planting, and digging irrigation ditches to water the fields.

With the acreage ready for planting, Tom and John were put in charge of planting and cultivating. They chose the best and most experienced 40 men who they knew would work hard and not complain. It took a month for the team to rework the ditches used to water the crops and begin planting.

The warden called Tom and John into his office and made both of them trustees. He put them in charge of the ranch. They began building a small farmhouse and the pens for the hogs and chickens. They had the workers fence off enough land for the cattle to graze. They assisted in building cattle pens for the milk cows. While working at the ranch a mule kicked Tom in the groin and he spent two weeks in the infirmary. He learned valuable nursing skills while he was recovering. Tom was anxious to get back to work on the ranch when he got out of the infirmary. John and three other prisoners had finished the farmhouse and several animal pens, during Tom's stay in the hospital. John, Tom and three other men finished all of the pens for the chickens, hogs, and goats by month's end. The next two months were spent digging postholes and fencing in 50 acres of state land for the cattle to graze. By July the crops were growing and the ranch was ready for all the livestock. The warden took John and Tom to Eloy to help him purchase the animals. He told John and Tom he was thrilled with the direction they had gone and was thankful for their hard work and all that they created. The warden said when they got back to the prison that he would provide a truck they could use to go back and forth to the ranch. He also wanted them to take a look at his home and make suggestions as to what plants he should buy. He asked them to take care of his yard and garden.

One of the ranch workers was a man named Willis Woods. Willis had a good friend, Barry Clemens, who was a bookkeeper at one of he banks in Florence and had known and worked with him for over twenty years. Willis Woods and Tom had done a lot of cattle business together.

One afternoon Barry came to the prison and visited the two of them at the prison ranch. He proposed that Woods and Tom escape and go to South America to take charge of several cattle ranches there that were owned by several U.S. banks.

Clemens told us he had made arrangements with a bank in Los Angeles to finance the deal. He said we were to look over the ranches and see if they were good for the bank to purchase. In addition, we were to supervise the operations of ranches the bank already owned and check on new ones for them to purchase. We were to get two-fifths of the profits each year for three years.

Tom wrote in his journal that he had been in prison for five years at that point in time; if he could get time off for good behavior he would never have made the break. But, he was in prison for the rest of his natural life and felt he had nothing to lose. He talked it over with John but John's health was not good and he was happy being a trustee and working on the ranch; he decided not to go.

Woods and Tom left the prison farm late the night of December 16th 1923. Barry Clemens and Charlie Journey were waiting for them in a car parked under some cottonwood trees about halfway between the prison and the ranch. They stayed at Journey's cotton ranch located near Chandler, Arizona for eight days while their travel arrangements were being made by Clemens. The cotton ranch was actually a front as Journey bootlegged whiskey. While they were at Journey's ranch they were visited by some friends including Charlie Beckham, a Florence deputy sheriff

A man named Bill Freeman was sent to pick them up for he next leg of their journey. He was to take them to Parker, Arizona. About 30 miles this side of Parker they met another deputy sheriff, who was to take them the rest of the way to Parker and to have them meet the banker from Los Angeles who made all the arrangements. The banker was to make sure they got to Los Angeles and board a ship to Argentina where a man named Smith was to meet them.

The deputy wanted to hide them in his house until he heard back from the Los Angeles' banker. Tom said they very suspicious and had the deputy take them to the nearby railhead where they caught a train to San Diego. Tom had friends they could stay with until the banker finished their travel arrangements.

Somehow the warden at the prison learned they were in San Diego. As it turned out that the whole South America thing was a big farce or at least something happened to make the deal fall through. In any event the warden wired the San Diego Police Chief informing him we were armed and dangerous and believed to be in the San Diego area.

The police had gained entrance, to the home where we were staying. by posing as electricians for the power company. Tom said;

> *"We were sitting in our shirtsleeves*
> *in the kitchen and were unarmed when*
> *a policeman drew his gun and*
> *announced we were under arrest."*

He realized at that point that we presented no danger so he told nearly a hundred policemen, waiting outside, they could leave. The policeman let us finish our dinner. He took us into custody and locked us up in the San Diego City Jail. On the ride to the jail the officer told us they were not sure they had the right people because we were unarmed and the pictures that were sent to them were very blurry.

The next morning two former wardens living in the area came to the jail and identified John and Tom. That was on January 23rd 1924 just about a month after our fruitless escape. A prison guard named Sam Hinton came to San Diego to return us to Florence. Hinton took us to the train station in San Diego and escorted us to Los Angeles where we transferred trains to the Southern Pacific line for the trip back to Florence. Tom figured the warden must have sent out an alarm indicating we were armed and dangerous because there were 29 officers waiting for us at the Los Angeles train depot. They looked quite surprised when the two of us stepped off the train with only one prison guard who had us handcuffed, but not shackled. Hinton just laughed and asked who they were waiting for with such a large posse of armed men. The officers never said a word, they just shook their heads, seeing Hinton had everything under control and left.

Woods and Tom got back to Florence a little after sunup and were sent to the Yard Office where Captain Reilly Brian took over. They were frisked and given cold showers and their heads were shaved. Both were taken to solitary confinement where they stayed for the next eight days while the warden decided their fate.

As soon as they were released Tom was escorted to the warden's office. The warden told Tom he needed him to go back to work with John at the ranch. If Tom promised not to escape again, he would be made a Trustee, so he could work side by side with his brother John. Tom said he didn't care about promising not to escape, but he needed the companionship of his brother. So Tom agreed to the warden's terms although he told the warden he wasn't sure if he could keep the promise not to escape.

In 1939, W.L. Wooten, a son of Bill Wooten, who was the deceased Kane Wooten's brother, came to work at the prison. Tom and John believed W.L. took the job with plans to kill them both and Tom Sisson.

W.L. was assigned to the northeast prison wall and carried a Thompson submachine gun. Tom said that he and John were not worried because they were trustees working at the prison ranch again. However, the captain of the guards moved Wooten, nicknamed "Braz" to the back wall of the prison. At this point Braz Wooten was way too close to where we were staying and it would be much easier for him to shoot us and claim we tried to escape.

We had overheard several of the guards talking about Braz Wooten, bragging how he planned to kill the Power brothers the minute he had a chance. We knew the warden would not listen to our accusations against Wooten. We decided we needed to escape if we had any hopes of staying alive. Soon after our decision, one night I saddled a horse and rode out to discuss our situation with a friend. I explained our suspicions and fears of Braz Wooten coming to work at the prison. Even before I finished my friend said;

> "We need to get you two out of there as soon as possible."

Tom goes on to say that he told the man that they would need a car that would get us to Yuma without stopping for gas. He told me he would take care of all the arrangements. He assured them that there would be some supplies and enough money left in the car to cover our expenses.

John wanted an old man he had befriended by the name of Bill Faultin to come with us. Bill was getting up in years and John wanted him to enjoy freedom in his final years. On the night of December 28th 1939, the three of us went up to the golf range where golfers teed off across the canal to a spot where the car was parked. We climbed in the car and headed for Yuma. We first stopped in Casa Grande to change into civilian clothes. Just below Somerton, Arizona, they left the car, fearing Yuma would be too obvious and too, it had a notorious prison.

We each had backpacks, along with a bed tarp and two big sheets wrapped up in them to be used for bedrolls. We had some groceries and three canteens of water. The three of us made our way to the Colorado River bottom, and headed south. We traveled along the river bottom for three days, making camp at night. On the evening of he third day, about 5 PM, we crossed the border into Old Mexico.

We later learned a Mexican patrol had come along the same area about twenty minutes after we had crossed the border. The patrolman who told me this said he heard on the radio about our escape three days earlier, but while we were in his country and if we behaved ourselves, he would not report us.

We had walked about three miles south of the border and spent the night in a thicket. The next day we came upon a house and bought an axe and a roll of barbed wire, for the purposes of building a raft to float down the Colorado River to the Gulf of California. Faulten and I had a difference of opinion about which logs to cut. I wanted to cut fallen dry logs, but Faulten insisted green logs would be better. We cut 39 green logs out of cottonwood and willow trees and assembled a raft.

We soon discovered our green-log-raft would not float; we should have used dry logs. This is where Faultin and we went our separate directions. Sometime many hours after our parting we saw a house built out in the middle of a cotton field. I climbed a nearby tree to take a look and see if there was any danger. While in the tree I spotted another house a few hundred yards beyond the house in the cotton field. John and I went to the first house to buy a chicken from the man, a woman and a girl who lived there, and they gave me a bit of lard. John and I made camp about fifty yards from their house, built a fire cooked the chicken and ate it; we slept there for the night.

The next day man in the house came by to check on us and pointed out that the second house was actually a store. I left John at the camp and walked down to the store to get some food, supplies, and water. When I entered the store I was confronted by a sheriff's posse of sixteen men. They arrested me on the spot, walked me back down to the camp and picked up John. However, the Mexican officers that were there took us into custody and brought us along with the sheriff's posse to San Luis. On the way, I bribed one of the Mexican officers for a hundred dollars to get us a car, some grub, and take us to Mexicali.

After we arrived at the San Luis police station I saw a familiar face. John Gleason, a member of the posse and a son of one of the officers who had traveled with us on the train from Los Angeles to Florence said, "I know that you bribed those men and if you will tell the Chief how much you gave them, I will get your money back for you." The $100 I had given the Mexican officer was immediately returned to me. From the Chief of Police's office. we were taken to the mayor's office. The first question the mayor asked us was;

> "Do you want to go back to the States? No. I said, Man, if I did, I would have stayed there in the first place."

One of the sheriff's, who arrested us in the store, was sitting in the mayor's office and spoke to the mayor saying;

"I thought you were going to let me take these boys back tonight?"

The Mayor responded;

"These men do not want to go back and the only way you can get them is to get a requisition for extradition form the District of the Federal Army in Mexico City."

The mayor concluded;

"I cannot hold them because they have not committed any crimes here in Mexico so I will be turning them loose in the morning."

We stayed there in San Luis with the Mexican soldiers for a month until they got orders to go to Mexicali to apprehend some prisoners that had escaped from prison. When the soldiers left we wasted no time and boarded a charter bus after dinner the same evening which took us to Santa Ana, a little over 500 miles south of San Luis. The trip by bus took several days and we became good friends with two bus drivers.

When we reached Santa Ana it was near suppertime. The bus driver dropped off the other passengers and took us to his house for dinner. After meeting his family and joining them for dinner the driver took us over to the train station so we could catch the train to Mazatlan. From there we rode the train to Guadalajara. A Mexican deputy sheriff came aboard the train and checked our papers that had been prepared for us at the mayor's office in San Luis. The train left from there and traveled east through the countryside, then it went south again and we arrived in Mexico City the next evening. Train travel in Mexico is very interesting. Families and individuals bring along their dogs, cats and even chickens and pigs. Needless to say it was hard to sleep, but the people were very friendly and shared their food.

From the train station, we took a taxi to the St. Regis Hotel and stayed there three days, until we learned our way around the town little better. We found an affordable apartment not far from the hotel where the landlady spoke a little English. We asked her about jobs and found out that we needed a work permit to legally work in Mexico. In our checking out the city we met a kind man who spoke English. He gave us a man's name in Acapulco who he said would hire us since we had told him our experiences as silver smiths. We caught a bus from Mexico City to Acapulco.

Arriving in Acapulco we met up with the man we were referred to by our friend in Guadalajara. He hired us on the spot and for a few months we worked for him making turquoise and silver jewelry. Tiring of trying to learn the language and Mexican way of life, we missed our friends in our own country and decided to head home. We boarded a train and got in late one night to Piedras Negras, a border town in Mexico, right across the border from Texas. After spending the night in a motel we walked around the next morning trying to figure out a plan to get back to the United States. The border was being watched closely by both the Mexican government and the U.S. Border Patrol looking for an escaped Mexican prisoner who was thought to be attempting his escape to the United States. We thought we found a safe place along the river where we could swim across late at night under the cover of darkness.

Just as we were wading out of the water on the U.S side of the river we were caught in a spotlight and approached by a border guard from about a hundred feet who was carrying what looked to be a pump shotgun. Another guard had spotted us from a tower along the U.S side of the border as we were swimming across. They had set a trap hoping to capture what they thought to be the escaped Mexican, but John and I walked right into their trap. The border patrol captain recognized us right off, he said;

"I know you two, you guys are hot!"

They put us in jail at Eagle Pass the American town across the border from Piedras Negras. The captain sent a wire to the warden at the Arizona State Prison, letting him know that Tom and John Power were in his custody, and they were to send officers to transport them back to the prison. While there in the jail a border official came to visit and asked us to go over the history of our arrest, trial and imprisonment. He said he was familiar with the whole story up until we got to Texas, He said;

"I know about this case, you men got a dirty deal."

He put us in touch with a lawyer, who explained to us he could get us released to the State of Texas, but we would never be able to leave Texas. He advised our best option would be to get the Arizona State Prison warden to promise in front witnesses that we would be pardoned and freed in a reasonable length of time.

The warden arrived at Eagle Pass a couple of days later with a prison guard. The warden promised in front of witnesses that John and I would be released after six months, the mandatory time for prisoners after being captured from an escape. With his signed promise to free us after six months, we decided our best course of action would be to trust the warden and return with him.

They left Eagle Pass that evening stopping about fifty miles from town when they came upon a restaurant in Del Rio, Texas. The warden and the guard decided to stop there for dinner; our handcuffs were and the warden bought us all a steak dinner. We rode all night on the way back to Florence, stopping only for coffee and restroom breaks. During the ride the warden informed us that Braz Wooten died of complications from the flu while we were on the lam. We were sorry to hear of his passing but we knew that we would be safe in prison.

I shared with the warden as we drove along an idea that came to me. I told him John and I had been working as silversmiths the past few months and suggested offering silversmith classes at the prison. This silversmith trade could provide a supplemental income for the prison by selling silver jewelry and related products. He perked right up hearing my suggestion and thought it would be a great idea. He pointed out it would keep the prisoners busy, teach them a trade, and agreed the prison could make extra income. He told us he would get the ball rolling as soon as we got the ranch back running up to snuff. He said during our absence it was not being run efficiently and that would be our first order of business.

Surprisingly we were not sent to solitary confinement when we got arrived back at the prison. The Yard Captain sent us to work in the flour mill explaining there were a lot of visitors coming to the prison over the next couple of weeks. The warden thought it best if John and I stayed out of sight for a while before we could
return to the ranch.

We got back to the prison on April 20th 1940 and after two weeks at the mill they transferred us to the ranch and made John and I trustee's again. Of course the warden did not honor his promise to have us released. The border patrol official wrote a series of letters to the warden expressing how disappointed he was that the warden did not keep his promise to secure our release from prison.

Warden Shute ignored all of the border official's requests, and the whole issue was forgotten. Warden Shute resigned in 1941.

A.G. Walker, the brother-in-law of Kane Wooten, was appointed the new warden in 1941. Approved by Walker, Dick Wooten, Kane's brother was hired as a guard. Leonard Wooten, Leonard was one of the late Braz Wooten's son. One can see evidences of Arizona's limited population, but an even clearer example of tight-knit family and community connections.

Dick Wooten was just as friendly to me as he had ever been. One evening John and I were walking along outside the east wall on the way to the pump house when Dick called out;

"Wait up, I want to talk to you."

He assured us if we needed anything, just come into the yard and get it. He kept his word. We were able to get anything we needed. Dick Wooten also became very good friends of Tom Sisson and visited with him on a regular basis, bringing him good home-cooked meals from time to time. Dick was so comfortable with and trusting of Sisson. The most amazing example I heard from Big Tom was the story he related to me. He told of the time Dick had shown Tom his Luger pistol. Tom had examined the gun and was surprised to find it fully loaded. I found this story even more remarkable knowing Dick was Kane Wooten's brother. And Kane was one of the officers killed in our old gun fight. His story reminded me how fortunate we three were. Here we were prisoners, convicted murderers yet so totally trusted and respected.

Another convincing example of not just the trust and respect, but something happening I was aware of but have no explanation for. When Leonard Wooten became Captain of the Yard, the first time he saw me and John in the yard, he waved us over told us he wanted to talk to us. Leonard quietly told us he had never done anything or said anything against us. He also offered to help us in anyway he could. This was the son of the same guy who hired on as a prison guard with full intentions to kill the three of us for revenge. Maybe there is something to what I've heard about time healing all wounds.

Tom and John's old friend Tom Sisson died in prison on January 23rd 1957 at the age of 86. Tom said again that Mr. Sisson was not guilty of any crime. But sadly he had to pay the penalty along with Tom and John because the people in authority were not going to leave him free to talk and tell what actually happened that day at the mine. Mr. Sisson did not die of any illness. He simply died of old age. For several years he hobbled around the prison with the aid of a crutch. He suffered from a bad case of arthritis. Tom and John checked on him while he was hospitalized to make sure he was being well cared for and see if there was anything he needed.

Just after Mr. Sisson died, the warden Walker sent for us to see what we wanted to do with Tom's body. We told the warden that Mr. Sisson wanted to be buried in a civilian cemetery. Tom's body was taken to an undertaker in Florence. John and I were taken to the mortuary to pick out a casket and headstone for him. Since Tom Sisson was a retired army veteran the government was supposed to pay for his burial costs, but that was not the case. John and Tom ended up paying the $510.00 to bury Big Tom.

Mr. Sisson had no living relatives and had willed his Army pension to my brother, John Power. Sadly, in all the times Tom's release came before the Parole Boards, each of the warden's testified that Tom should not be paroled because he was too old to work. However, the truth was Mr. Sisson had saved money from his pension that was in excess of $10,000. Along with the interest from his savings and his monthly pension Tom would have been able to sustain a comfortable life in the outside world.

What follows is a diversion from the established chronological time line and narrative format, the author's goal is to present the historical information and background evidence of this remarkable piece of Arizona history, along with a clearer and more accurate depiction of the plight of the Power Brothers and Mr. Tom Sisson. The reader, though, shall be the one to determine innocence or guilt as it pertains to The Power Affair, based on all the information provided by the author in this book.

Chapter Fifteen

On November 24th 1926 the Power brothers submitted their first application to the Board of Pardons and Paroles in Florence. They based their petition on the fact that they did not get a fair trial. Their application was denied based on a letter that was sent to the board by W.R. Chambers, Judge in the Superior Court who was the States County Attorney who had prosecuted them at their trial. In a nutshell he said in the letter that the Power brothers and Tom Sisson had a fair trial. Based on the letter their petition for parole was denied.

Their next effort to gain their freedom came in June of 1935, at which they invited around thirty of their friends to attend the meeting of the State Board of Pardons and Paroles. As always, Jay Murdock was among those attending. Both Tom and John appeared confident of achieving their aim of receiving their release. Tom was neatly dressed in civilian clothes, and was in charge of the proceedings. He arranged a tempting dinner to be served to his friends in the officers' mess hall. At the board meeting Tom made a strong plea to have their sentences reduced to twenty years. This would have left them with only a short remaining time to serve, by including their time off for good behavior.

At the hearing Jay Murdock and others spoke on behalf of the men. The most convincing words were spoken by Rome Haby, the son of Mr. and Mrs. Haby owners of the Haby ranch. He emphasized the fact that both Tom and John had been good neighbors and law abiding citizens. Dick Elwood, who played a part in the history of the Power mine, also spoke well of them, telling of his association as a onetime share owner with the Power family. A letter from Judge Lain stated, the three men had been poorly represented at their trial. Sadly, their plea for a pardon was doomed to disappoint once again; their application for parole was denied.

Their next hearing before the Parole Board was on December 17th 1952. An attorney, Wilford R. Richardson, had been hired by the same people who had put them away 34 years before. Richardson said, among other things, that the Powers had established a fort in the mountains to take on any officers that came after them. He informed the board that Tom and John built barricades at the cabin. His testimony was the end of that hearing.

At that point the Power brothers knew they were doomed to spend the rest of their lives in prison. They knew that for many years they had made many suggestions and worked hard to improve many conditions that benefited the prison but also helped line the pockets of the wardens. They knew the wardens were not about to let their cash cows out of prison.

Sadly, the Power brothers were not allowed to speak on their own behalf. It was later discovered what was said to be a "fort" in the mountains was simply a cave that the family had used whiled working two mining claims in the area, nearly six miles from their cabin. Those finding and searching the cave discovered some canned food and a couple cots that the Powers had used when they worked their claims. It turned out both claims were worthless so they abandoned the cave. And as far as their cabin being barricaded, well a simple visit to their cabin would have showed this statement to be preposterous. They had no idea that they were "slackers" until Lieutenant Hayes took them into custody at the border and informed them that they were wanted for draft dodging. That was the first time they realized why the officers came to their cabin; it was to arrest them. They ran after the gun battle because three officers were killed and they knew that their lives were not worth a plug nickel.

In 1958, a reporter from the Arizona Republic, Don Dedera, wrote a series of articles about their case. He came to the prison to interview Tom Power. He told Tom he wanted a story. Tom asked him;

> *"Are you going to write one article and then run off and hide?"*

Don told Tom;

> *"I'm no quitter."*

Tom said he sat down and told Don the whole story. He said the reporter listened carefully and took notes, but Tom could see by the reporter's body language that he did not believe him.

Dedera's first article about the Powers, reported that their father was a domineering man and that after the deaths of their mother and sister, he had vowed not to lose any more of his kin;

> *"The Power boys wanted to join up."*

his column read. This was a statement that Jeff Power supposedly said to one of his friends. Tom said that the statement was never verified and should not have been quoted by the reporter. He further reported in this article that;

> *"The eldest son ran off to Safford and joined a cavalry outfit that went overseas in the fall of 1917."*

The article further stated that their father, Jeff Power had disowned him. Actually, Charlie Power left their home in the Gulaiuro Mountains in 1915 to go to New Mexico. In point of fact, the country had not entered war at that time. Charlie later married and fathered four children, three boys and a girl.

Tom said he did learn something new from that first article. He found out an uncle of theirs had offered to lead Deputy Marshal Haynes safely to the Power cabin to avoid violence, and Haynes turned down his offer. Tom was not sure but he thought it might have been their Uncle Wily Morgan. Tom believed Uncle Wiley, or anyone could have led the officers to the cabin without any danger.

Dedera also reported that the Power family had been feuding with the Wooten family;

> *"Some folks said that one of the Wooten family was sweet on their sister Ola Power but she spurned him before she died. Others say the two families made claim to the same grazing lands."*

Tom Power wrote in his journal that their father, Jeff Power, was a calm, fun loving, jovial man and he had no trouble with anybody. He definitely had no feud with the Wooten family. They were good neighbors and both families' cattle herds grazed together sharing the same government land for many years. Tom said Ola did not date any of the Wooten brothers, but if she had, Tom went on to say their father would have considered that her business and would not have interfered. There was no trouble between the Wooten family and the Power family, except the time they caught Tim and his brother rounding up the Power cattle. Tom said there was no way that any of their brushes with the Wooten family would have been reason for them to kill anyone. Gold fever and/or greed may have been underlying reasons for the shooting.

When questioned about the mysterious death of his sister Ola, Tom simply said it was a dirty deed and that the guy who was the cause knew who he was. He further indicated that their father took their sister to several doctors and she was treated for neck and upper back pain after the buggy accident that took the life of their grandmother. Tom did not go into detail but he indicated that he blamed the neighbor who loaned his grandmother and sister a wild horse to pull their buggy the day they came to bring the men their lunches. The horse got spooked and went out of control causing the buggy to flip over instantly killing their grandmother and causing the serious injury to their sister, that eventually killed her.

The columnist, Don Dedera, recounted the story about the crime and the subsequent manhunt. However, he had based his information on the newspaper articles from around the state in 1918. He repeated some of the testimony of the only survivor of the gunfight on the officers' side, Deputy Marshal Haynes, but he failed to note the inconsistencies in his testimony.

To Dedera's credit he later began checking the records that were available and started to notice these and other inconsistencies. From that point he stared to point out many of the incorrect statements found in many testimonies of the witnesses. He really stirred up a lot of controversy with the people whose main goal in life was to keep Tom and John Power along with Tom Sisson locked up in prison.

Don received many letters from relatives of the dead officers indicating they wanted to keep the brothers in jail because they feared of their lives if the boys got out of jail. The relatives of one of the dead officers wrote and told Dedera to look at the record. Don wrote in the next article that he had looked at the record, and he reported again the testimony of Deputy Marshal Haynes before the coroner's jury. One of the slain officers' relatives wrote him back and said;

> "Deputy Marshal Frank Haynes was an unreliable witness and everyone knew that. Haynes told several stories before the trial and contradicted himself on the witness stand."

Dedera reminded the readers again that he had looked very thoroughly at the records and he reported again;

> *"It is 41 years too late to begin doubting the truthfulness of Frank Haynes. Especially since his testimony, principally, put the Power brothers in prison."*

Our friend, Lee Solomon spoke with Don Dedera, Bill Wooten, T.K. Wooten's father, who was married to his Lee's sister. Lee told Dedera about his conversation with T.K. Wooten just a few days before the shootout, in which T.K. told Lee, that he was going to go up to the mine and shoot the hell out of the Power family and get their mine. It must be noted though, "Kane" Wooten was a notorious boaster, and was known to be full of hot air. In any event there was no doubt that Sheriff Frank McBride would have had any part in any dirty deed against the Power brothers. He had been a friend of the Power family from the time before he was elected the Sheriff of Graham County. Tom and John campaigned across the county during Frank McBride's election and Frank offered Tom the job as his undersheriff after he was elected and again Tom turned down the job.

Reporter Dedera further checked the records at the prison and devoted one article to the hearing that was grated to them on December 17th 1952, after they had been in prison for more than 34 years. At that Parole Board meeting more than 20 relatives of the slain officers appeared at the meeting to protest their release. At the hearing, a former superior court judge brought in a written protest bearing the names of 104 folks from in and around Safford. There were also written protests from another judge, a justice of the peace, and an attorney. One of the victims had a brother-in-law who explained the whole county feared for their lives if the Power brothers and Sisson were freed. Nobody spoke on behalf of Power brothers other than Lee Solomon who simply told the board any threats to the people would have been complete insanity. In fact, he said that the Power brothers and Tom Sisson couldn't hurt a flea. Sadly, the prison warden said nothing, perhaps because he was not about to lose his retirement investment.

Dedera noted that the odds against commutation of their sentence were enormous. The people from the Safford group moved to squelch each of the Power requests for freedom. It was a fact that most of the officials at the prison believed the Powers and Sisson deserved a break. The warden even had the boys work at his place babysitting his children and taking care of his lawn and garden. This certainly indicated the Power brothers were not a threat to anyone. At that point Dedera realized it would be an uphill battle to get them released because there was still so much negativity attached to them.

Don Dedera wanted to set the record straight and wrote seven articles starting on November 9th 1958 and running to November 16th 1958. He started the ball rolling to get the Power brothers and Tom Sisson released from prison. These articles proved to be the main reason why they were eventually released and received a full pardon.

The first article written and published by reporter Don Dedera was on November 9th 1958 that appeared in the Arizona Republic newspaper;

Good morning Arizona

The Power brothers are in their 41st year at the state prison in Florence, Arizona, which is the longest term served in the state. They are mild-mannered, old, hardworking men who succor their spirits with the hope that some day they will be free. Unrelenting hatred, political cowardice, and paternal, bureaucratic affection keep's them there in prison. They probably will die there. "Why reopen the Power case?" Many folks have asked me. "It's ancient history. It ought to be forgotten." And I wonder why? Why should it be hidden away and avoided and hushed up?

Arizona justice has demanded more time from the Powers than from any other criminals. Shouldn't this case be worthy of holding out to our children as our grandest example of government law? The record is open, for anyone who cares to ask and look. I went to the Power brothers, to the prison records, to the state archives, to newspapers of that day, to a book written about the Power case, to people who saw the trial, and to surviving friends and enemies of the Power family.

I've tried hard to get at the truth, and after 41 years, truth may be out of reach. But there's no disputing this: nearly 20,000 criminals have been imprisoned, and most released, since the Powers were confined. Thomas and John Power were convicted of first degree murder by a jury at Clifton in May 1918. They were found guilty of murdering the Graham County sheriff and two of his deputies.

They were sentenced to life terms on May 20th, 1918, and were delivered to the prison on May 22nd. Except for brief escapes, they have remained there since. At the time of their imprisonment, John was 27 and Tom 25. Both were described as being unmarried cowpunchers. Tom ran away from a trusty gang on December

1st 1923, and was recaptured in San Diego on January 24th, 1924. When questioned about the break, Tom said, "I had it in my mind to go to South America and start me a cattle business, but the men who helped me escape spilled the beans and told the officers exactly where to find me."

The brothers escaped together on December 28th, 1939, and four months later were trapped near the Mexican border. They escaped from prison, the brothers said, because a brother of one of the victims was hired as a prison guard. Tom said, "He was walking the wall with a "tommy gun" and we heard through the grapevine that he was planning on killing us. So we went to the warden to tell him we were worried about our lives. He told us that the man did not work at the prison. When the guard was moved to the back wall, which overlooked the prison ranch where we lived we knew our days were numbered so we decided our best bet was to escape."

Those escapes are the only bad marks on the Power records for nearly 41 years. They have worked at every job at the prison, from road building to blacksmithing. Today they nighthawk prison cattle, and tend the horses of the mounted guards. They are entrusted to stay in their own cabin outside the prison walls. On the average, an Arizona life term is commuted after 10 or 12 years. Yet the Power brothers have served more than 40 years. Why? Was their crime so heinous, so premeditated, and so vicious *that society could never punish them too much?*

Below is the next article written and published by reporter Don Dedera on November 10th 1958 in the Arizona Republic.

Good Morning Arizona

America was at war with the Central Powers. T.J. Power was at war with the people around him. Old Jeff, as his neighbors called him, was obstinately independent. He was domineering and he had more than his share of grief. His wife was killed when she was buried under a collapsed adobe roof. His mother was killed in a riding accident and his only daughter, whom he loved so dearly, died of a mysterious illness. Old Jeff turned his attentions to his boys, Bud (Charles), John and Tom. The Power family came to Arizona from Texas and New Mexico. They settled for a while in Klondyke and staked out mining and grazing claims in the Galiuro Mountains in southwestern Graham County. Old Jeff Power, lonesome for someone his age, made friends with a retired army scout, Tom Sisson. Sisson became a business partner and member of the family.

In 1917, as the United States was preparing its greatest effort against Germany, the newspapers in Safford, Clifton and Miami were filled with reports of heroism and atrocities. A young man out of uniform needed to have a good excuse. The Power brothers wanted to join up. "I'll see you in hell first!" ranted Old Jeff. "This country shouldn't be throwing away the lives of our sons on foreign soil." Bud, the eldest son, ran off to Safford and jointed a cavalry outfit and went overseas in the fall of 1917. Old Man Power disowned his son. Bud's name was never mentioned again by him. He redoubled his hold on his remaining sons.

Draft evasion has been offered as a single motive for the terrible killings which followed. But there were other, more-subtle factors. For years the Power family had been feuding with the Wooten family. Some say one of the Wooten brothers was sweet on Ola Power, Jeff's daughter, but she spurned him. Others say the two families made claim on the same grazing lands. Whatever the reason, there was bad blood between the Wooten's and the Powers' especially between Kane Wooten, a deputy sheriff, and young Tom Power. Down in the valley, citizens were demanding action against slackers. What about the Power boys?

The duty fell to Frank Haynes, U.S. deputy marshal of the district covering northeastern Arizona. Haynes himself, before he died, admitted that better judgment on his part might have averted the tragedy. What he did was swear out a warrant for the arrest of the Power boys. Their uncle Wily Morgan heard about the warrants. He offered to lead Haynes safely to the Power cabin in the mountains. But Haynes turned down that offer. Instead, he accepted the help volunteered by Sheriff Robert F. McBride and Deputies Martin Kempton and Kane Wooten.

On the night of February 9th, 1918, the four officers went to serve the warrants. They arrived by car into the Galiuros', borrowed horses from their neighbor, and rode up Rattlesnake Canyon through a blinding snowstorm. Four went up the canyon. One came back alive, and the stories he told inflamed a whole state against those uneducated, backwoods boys.

The next article written by Dedera was published in the Arizona Republic was on November 11th 1958.

Good Morning Arizona

Why county peace officers went along to serve a federal warrant is a great mystery of the Power case. Frank Haynes, U.S. deputy marshal, turned down a chance to be escorted safely by a Power relative. Haynes wasn't a dude. A former sheriff, he had brought in hundreds of bad men single-handed, without firing a shot. But Haynes accepted the help of Robert F. McBride, Graham County Sheriff, and two of his deputies, Mart Kempton and Kane Wooten. The three county officers were eager to go.

Haynes was the posse's only survivor. Later he told, with some contradiction, the basic story: "After holding consultation, it was decided that Wooten and Kempton should take the front corners of the house and that McBride and myself should bring up the rear." Haynes repeatedly said he couldn't see what happened up front, and soon lost track of Wooten. The cabin was two rooms made of logs with a couple of small windows, a stone fireplace, and a canvas door. Haynes heard some shouting, then a burst of gunfire, and then things became very confusing.

Haynes, the man with the warrant, never identified himself to the occupants of the cabin, didn't ask for them to give up, didn't fire a shot, and didn't see the fight. He rode away for help. Two men living today know how the fight started. A jury did not believe them. But John and Tom Power have sworn to their version without change for nearly 41 years. They say they were asleep when the officers surrounded their cabin. Inside were John, Tom, Old Jeff and Tom Sisson, the former Indian scout.

Dawn was just breaking. They woke when a belled mare ran past the front of the cabin. Old Jeff, thinking a mountain lion was after the mare, stepped outside dressed in long johns and carrying his rifle. "Throw up your hands!" Shouted Kane Wooten from around the corner, "Don't shoot!" said old Jeff Power. He put down his rifle and raised his arms, the brothers and the Haynes say. As he did, the Power brothers believe, Kane Wooten shot old Jeff Power through one of his lungs. John Power said he dashed outside unarmed to aid his father. Wooten fired at him and missed. John Power dived back inside and grabbed up his rifle.

"Our father was shot down in cold blood," said Tom Power. "We didn't have any idea who it was that was outside. All we knew was that our father was shot, and they were trying to kill us. What would you have done?" Within the next few *moments, the Power boys said, they fired a total of five shots. They think their bullets killed Wooten and Kempton. To this day they swear Tom Sisson crawled under his bed and didn't fire a shot. Sheriff McBride, they believe, was killed by a stray Kane Wooten slug.*

They said that, according to a coroners' finding, McBride was struck by a .30 caliber bullet. Tom Power said John was using a .41 caliber rifle and Tom was shooting a .35 caliber rifle. Their father was the only one in their family that shot a .30 caliber rifle and Deputy Marshal Haynes has sworn he saw that gun lying next to Jeff Power's body. Both Power boys were cut by bullet-shattered glass, and both lost the sight of their left eyes. The deed was done. Society never forgave their next action

The next article that was written by Dedera was published in the Arizona Republic Newspaper on November 12th 1958.

Good morning Arizona

If the Power boys had stayed to face their accusers, they might have been exonerated. Or they might have been lynched. A sheriff and two deputies were dead outside their cabin. Their father, who had ordered them to evade the draft, lay dying. The Power boys got help for their father from neighbors, saddled up their horses, and lit out for Mexico, with Tom Sisson as their guide. Jay Murdock, a neighbor, later had some interesting things to say about Old Jeff Power's fatal wound. It was in the chest, penetrating a lung. The wound would not bleed when the old man held his breath, but when he breathed; blood came up through the pectoral muscle.

Once Old Jeff Power raised his arms, blood came out like a geyser. Murdock deducted that for the hole in the muscle and lung to have been made by the same bullet, Old Man Power's arms must have been raised above his head. For 26 days the Power boys and Sisson eluded the largest manhunt in Arizona history. At one time 3,000 men were on their trail, including five troops of cavalry. The fugitives slipped into and through the Chiricahuas, and across the border. On March 8th, 1918, they surrendered to the sixth United States Cavalrymen 12 miles below the border near Hachita, New Mexico. When they gave up without a shot, the Power boys and Tom Sisson handed over three rifles, two pistols, and 600 rounds of ammunition. "What better proof that we weren't dangerous criminals?" said Tom Power the other day, "We didn't have to give up. All the time we were running we were looking for authorities who wouldn't kill us first and ask questions later."

The Power boys don't quibble about the illegal invasion of Mexico by American troops. Even, today, along the border, kidnapping is practiced as the quickest form of extradition. The fugitives were brought the military post at Hachita, and the new Graham county sheriff, Brig Stewart, returned them to Safford. That feeling was high against them is beyond dispute. *They were slackers. And the country was at war.*

The Newspapers described them as slack-jawed, insane half-breeds who mutilated the bodies of the men they killed for pleasure. Yet U.I. Paxton, justice of the peace and coroner, reported that Sheriff McBride was shot in the head and knee, Kempton once through the neck, and Kane Wooten once through the back. Only one bit of mutilation evidence did Paxton submit. Across Kane Wooten's face, put there after death, was the imprint of a man's shoe.

Once while the Power boys and Sisson were in the Safford jail, Howard McBride, the brother of the dead sheriff, asked to interview the prisoners. A pistol was taken from him when he was searched before entering the holding cell of the men. "I'm glad you did that," he told jailer Dave Skaggs. "If you hadn't, I would be in jail instead of them." Believing they would never find 12 unbiased jurors in Safford, lawyers for the Powers and Sisson asked for and received a change of venue to Clifton, in Greenlee County, 30 miles away. Even then, some interesting evidence wasn't heard.

The next article written and published by Don Dedera appeared in the Arizona Republic on November 13th 1958.

Good morning Arizona

The Power boys claim they were railroaded by a stacked jury, an unfair judge, perjured testimony, and inept counsel. Little basis for such a harsh conclusion can be found in the reports of their trial. Much of society had judged them guilty before the trial began. But the Power boys were given their rights. To begin with, they were granted a change of venue from prejudiced Safford, to Clifton, county seat of Greenlee County.

Judge Frank B. Lain had a reputation for impartiality. The jury was chosen in a day, indicating the well-paid Power lawyers had no trouble picking jurors with professed open minds. The jury consisted of: E.A. Wood, painter, Clifton; Sam Sloan, cattleman, Apache Creek; C.A. Lennox, miner, Metcalf; George R. Kiddie, assayer, Morenci; J.E. Dart, Metcalf; C.M. Staples, accountant, Morenci; S.F. Spriggs, purchasing agent, Clifton; C.M. Bishop, construction foreman, Clifton; J.H. Goolsby, smelter superintendent, Clifton; T.N. Brown, farmer, Duncan; J.V. Lippets Carpenter, Morenci; and Dan Grant, miner, Morenci.

Frank Haynes, U.S. deputy marshal and the only posse survivor, was the chief witness for the state. Haynes repeated in detail how he and the Graham officers sneaked up on the cabin during darkness and waited for dawn. Again Haynes admitted he was behind the cabin, where he couldn't see the beginning of the fight, yet he testified: "The first shots came from the east door of the cabin, and Jeff Power fell as soon as the shots were fired. I don't know who shot Old Man Power." Perhaps the greatest injustice of the trial was the gagging of Jay Murdock, a witness for the defense. Murdock, neighbor of the

Powers, had been called to care for the dying Jeff Power.

Defense lawyers contended the fight started when Kane Wooten shot down Old Man Power as Power's hands were raised. The argument was the foundation of the defense. "And what did T.J Power tell you before he died?" a defense attorney asked Murdock. "Objection!" shouted the prosecutor. The objection was sustained.

The jury never heard the dying declaration of Old Man Jeff Power: "I can't see why Kane Wooten shot me with my hands up." Other potent defense arguments were ignored.

The boys were dominated by a possessive father. They were ignorant, unlettered mountain boys who didn't know their obligation to register for the draft. The arrest was attempted when bad light made identification difficult. In the posse was a man with a personal grudge against the Powers. And if, as the prosecutor charged, the Power bunch had set an ambush for the officers, why was Old Man Power dressed in his long underwear on a snowy winter morning? Why hadn't the Power boys removed the dangerous glass from the windows from where they fought? Why had the posse been allowed to reach the corners of the cabin, the best attacking fighting points?

The jury retired. They considered the case of draft-dodgers who admitted killing a sheriff and two deputies. A guilty verdict against them and Tom Sisson was returned in 30 minutes. Capital punishment had been outlawed in Arizona, and so the Power boys and Sisson got life terms.

Below is the next article in Don Dedera's series regarding the Power Affair that was published in the Arizona Republic newspaper on November 14, 1958.

Good morning Arizona

The Power brothers asked two favors of me. First, "Please spell our name right," said Tom, "It's Power. Not Powers. I guess there have been thousands of stories about us, but nobody ever asked us how we spell our name." John broke in the conversation, "And don't say we've had a dozen chances at parole." Under Arizona Law, a lifer can't be paroled. His only chance is a clemency hearing. The state board of pardons and paroles may commute a life term to time served. The Power case never was appealed to the Supreme Court. John and Tom Power along with Tom Sisson petitioned time and again for a board hearing. The petitions were not considered favorably, if at all, until they had served 34 years.

The actual hearing was granted on December 17th 1952. Appearing against the Powers and Sisson were more than 20 relatives of the slain officers. Tom described them as, "Little kids just hatched out. Mother's who weren't even born when we were put in prison; old men, who were 30 miles away from our cabin at the time of the shooting." A former superior judge brought in a list of 104 Safford names, protesting our release, along with other written protests *from a justice of the peace, an attorney, a brother-in-law of one of the, and from American Legion posts at Safford and Ajo.*

The parole board did not free the Powers and Sisson. The prisoners failed at their one and only hearing. The case has not been reheard since. Tom Sisson, at 86, the oldest state prisoner, died January 23rd, 1957, and left $10,000 saved from his army pension to John Power. "There was never a bad mark on Sisson's record here," said the prison official. Last summer, J.F. Weadcock of the Arizona Daily Star, made an extensive investigation of the Power case. He wrote: "The facts seem to say that Old Jeff Power, in his stubborn attitude toward the draft, coupled with Kane Wooten's desire for vengeance for some reason or another, juggled the two boys into a mess which was not of their making," in favor of the Power boys.

Reasonable doubt that they were guilty of first-degree murder. Draft evaders, they were convicted of murder at a time of patriotic fever. Although heavily armed, they gave up without a fight to a cavalry patrol they could have easily exterminated, and during their imprisonment and escapes, have not committed a single crime against society. But the odds against commutation are enormous. The Safford group has moved to squelch every Power petition for leniency. And the officials who now believe the Powers deserve a break doubt that freedom for the Power brothers would be good: "They are old men, imprisoned too long. They couldn't take care of themselves on the outside. Here they have a good home, good food, and medical care." The Power boys were put in prison to protect society. Now, it seems, the Power boys are kept in prison to protect themselves from society.

Below is the next article written by Don Dedera that was published in the Arizona Republic on November 16th 1958;

Good Morning Arizona

Many relatives of the victims of the shooting at the Power mine believe they know what happened there the morning of Sunday February 10th, 1918. They say I've got it all wrong. "Every 3 or 4 years someone starts a campaign to get them paroled or pardoned," states one letter. "So far, members of the families of the murdered men [one of the men was Don Dedera's brother-in-law have managed to keep Tom and John Power in prison. "We hope to continue to do so. And should they be pardoned, we will make every effort possible to send them back for the murder of one of the other officers. They were tried only for the murder of one of the officers."

All of the dead men were married. They left large families, and understandably, feeling against the Power brothers, the Graham officers were murdered heroes. They did no wrong. Relatives have been calling and posting letters to me all week. They charge: Kane Wooten was the first man shot, while he was still on his horse. Sheriff McBride was *the first man shot. Haynes, the U.S. deputy marshal, was authorized and ordered to deputize a large posse to bring in the Power brothers.*

The posse was ambushed, while it was at some distance from a barricaded, fortified cabin. Further, Kane Wooten had no personal interest in lands near the Power mine. "Look at the record," demand the relatives. I have looked at the record, including the sworn testimony only delivered before a coroner's jury by Frank Haynes, the sole survivor of the posse. By his own testimony, still on record in Safford: Old Jeff Power was the first man shot. Haynes was authorized to take only one man with him to arrest the Powers, and the others begged to go. The Posse by sneaking up before dawn on foot, managed to reach within 10 feet of the front door before the inhabitants of the cabin, first Old Man Jeff Power, knew they were there, Old Jeff stepped outside in his underwear. Window glass had not been removed. No portholes had been cut by the defenders.

Kane Wooten definitely had an interest in a cattle ranch near the Power mine. These are the statements of Deputy U.S. Marshal Frank Haynes and not this reporter and are on the official record, open to the friends and enemies of the Power brother. "Frank Haynes was an unreliable witness," said one relative of Mart Kempton. "Everyone knew that. He told several stories before the trial, and contradicted himself on the witness stand." Its 41 years too late to begin doubting the truthfulness of Deputy Marshal Frank Haynes. His testimony, principally, put the Power brothers in prison.

Don Dedera of the Arizona Republic and Bob Thomas of the Tucson Daily Examiner were personably responsible for bringing the Power brothers' case before the public again after 41 years with the idea of righting a very long overdue wrong. Because of the diligence of these two men, many people around the state learned about their plight for the first time. The public finally had a chance to read about the shooting from both sides. Sentiment finally began to sway in favor of the Power brothers and Tom Sisson instead of the truth being buried by folks in Graham County.

A second hearing before the Parole and Pardon's board was held in March of 1960. To the benefit of the prisoners the new chairman of the board was an unbiased Reverend Walter Hoffman. The parole board at that time consisted of three members including Reverend Hoffman, W.W. "Skipper" Dick, the Arizona State Superintendent of Instruction; and Wade Church, the Arizona State Attorney General. At this hearing the Reverend Hoffman began by bringing up all the things that had been used so effectively against John and Tom in the past; he dwelt upon the horrible killings of the law officers, and the cowardly *"slacking" of the Power brothers.*

"Wait a minute."

Said Wade Church. The room became completely still; then he spoke out loud saying;

. *"Did the officers identify themselves before the shooting started?"*

Church asked. Reverend Hoffman was the first person to answer;

*"No, not according to the trial
records nor in any other record that
can be found or have been presented."*

Following Hoffman, W.W. "Skipper" Dick, who was
soon to be a very influential politician in Arizona, the
prison parole clerk and the then current warden of the
prison, Frank Eyman all said that the officers had not
identified themselves before the shooting took place;

*"Then the shooting of a man with
his hands up, referring to Old Man Jeff
Power, was nothing but cold blooded
murder,"*

Arizona State Attorney General Wade Church
went on to say;

*"I'd have killed every one of the
sons of bitches,"*

After the hearing, Wade Church came up to Tom
and John and put his hands on their shoulders and
said;

*"Don't throw away any more time or
money on your defense, Church went
on to say, We're going to get you two
boys out of here."*

Several more newspaper articles were written
over the next two years by Don Dedera of the Arizona
Republic and Bob Thomas continuing to bring the
plight of the brothers in front of the public eye and
presenting evidence on record indicating the brothers
were given a dirty deal.

The Power brothers' greatest defender at that
point was the State Attorney General Wade Church,
who made it his undivided attention to look at all the
records, testimony and copies of all inquests. After
completing his research, Church realized without a
doubt, that the Power brothers did not receive a fair
trial and that they were railroaded. Church went on to

make it his mission to obtain a complete release from prison for Tom and John Power.

Then on April 16th 1960, a little over 42 years after a posse shot it out with a hard-nosed mining and cattle family on Sunday February 10th 1918, in remote Rattlesnake Canyon in the Galiuro Mountains southwest of Safford, Arizona, in the most famous gunfight since the gunfight at the O.K. Corral on October 18th, 1881, that next Wednesday after the hearing in March of 1960, at the Arizona State Prison in Florence, the only living participants in the gun battle will have another parole board hearing. The hearing was to determine if the 42 years the Power Brothers had spent behind bars was enough punishment for defending themselves, against a posse who had first fired upon them and resulted in four men killed.

Some relations of the old posse say it isn't, and that the Power brothers, John, at that time age 70 and his brother Tom, age 68 should serve out their life sentences. The board adjourned to consider all of the testimony presented at the hearing. They reconvened on April 20th, 1960. John and Tom Power appeared again before the Pardon and Parole board.

Lorenzo Wright, an ex-warden of the prison, was the first one to address the board. He spoke three times on behalf of Tom and John Power. When he finished his talks, he asked Tom to get up and speak, stating it was about time he had the opportunity to speak after 42 years. Tom stood up and began;

> "I've been waiting a long time for a chance to do that."

When began to speak several people attending the hearing started making noise. They pounded on the steel tables in the room until a person couldn't have heard it thunder. When the disturbance was quelled, Tom was able tell his and John's side of the story, giving a detailed explanation of the facts surrounding the shooting; he sat down.

The next to speak was Ted Mullin, another ex-warden, who spoke on behalf of the Power brothers. Then Glen L. Randall, an attorney from Mesa also spoke on their behalf. Randall had been one of the lawyers that Tom and John consulted while they were in prison. He said;

> *"You people are all good Christians; God-loving people, if you cannot forgive on this earth, how do you expect to be forgiven in the next life?"*

Wilford R. Richardson, the attorney from Safford, was the only person who spoke against the brothers. He said, as he pointed to the widows of Sheriff McBride and his deputy Mart Kempton;

> *"If you turn these two men loose,"* pointing at John and Tom where they sat, *"these two widows back here won't be able to sleep at night."*

When Richardson finished, Tom Power got up to speak. He was prepared to burn Richardson down. He came armed with law books, and pictures of the cabin where the infamous battle had taken place 42 years before. First off, Tom was going to ask Richardson to show the folks at the hearing the barricades that surrounded the Power cabin, he had testified he saw in 1952. It would have been impossible for him to accuse the brothers of removing the barricades or of changing anything at the cabin since John and Tom had been in prison since 1918 and had no way of moving the barricades.

Next Tom wanted to show Richardson the penalty in the law books for draft evasion, which, if convicted would have been fifteen to ninety days in jail. He wanted to point out that it would be ludicrous to believe that we would have risked their lives to keep from serving a 90-day sentence. Tom said he decided to depart from the prepared talk. He simply faced the people and said;

"We ask your forgiveness for shooting the men and that we were sorry for the deaths of the officers and our father. We ask the widow's and their families for their forgiveness for the loss of their husbands and loved ones."

At the conclusion of the hearing, Reverend Hoffman, announced that John and Tom Power would be released. He asked that the room be cleared of spectators so the necessary business could be concluded. John and Tom Power tried to leave the room, but Tom says they could hardly move because of the people who were stopping them to offer congratulations, or to shake hands with them. The new Captain of the Guards kept trying to clear the room, but without much success.

Below is the next article written by Don Dedera regarding Tom and John Power's fight to obtain their release from prison, that appeared in the Arizona Republic Newspaper, in Dedera's column called Good Morning Arizona, on November 24th 1967.

For 18 months I have been harping on the Power case, and now that the old brothers have won their freedom and I can't contain my sentiment. The 42-year captivity of the Powers was a shame of Arizona justice. Their release should be a state pride. For last week Arizonans were equal to the challenge. Citizens from the highest elected official to just plain country folks displayed varieties of that precious human quality, courage. It took a kind of courage for people to come from Graham County to oppose the release of the brothers, and it took a kind of courage for a family to come from Tonto Basin to favor it. The Reverend Walter Hoffman had the courage to bring up the case. He had the courage to insist on dignity, and the courage to hear all reasonable argument.

Wilford R. Richardson, the lawyer speaking against the Power brothers showed courage in restraint. He wasn't only a paid attorney, but he was also a man who believed in his cause. But even in defeat his was the courage of a gentleman. Lee Solomon had the courage to drive from Kirkland Junction to look any man in the eye and swear he was a witness to the feuding that led up to the shooting. Ted Mullin, himself a law officer, and Alva Weaver, long a Pinal County Official, had the courage to plead for mercy for Tom and John Power who were convicted of killing three law officers.

Touching everyone at the hearing was the courage of Lorenzo Wright, the leader of the Mormon Church in Maricopa County, who related to the two families of the Powers' victims, beseeching his kinfolk to relent. And then, Wright reached a fresh height of courage when he abandoned the Power brothers. He put the question squarely up to them, to forgive and ask forgiveness.

How much courage did the Powers have? Tom had come to the hearing with his annotated law books, his cross-indexed news clippings, his dog-eared letters, prepared to argue the right and wrong of the furious gun battle that took *place 42 years ago. But he found within himself the courage to say the only words that anybody wanted to hear: "We will forgive, and would like to be forgiven." Perhaps of a greater struggle was wrought the courage of John Power. Those who knew him would more expect San Francisco Peaks to topple into Lake Mary than to hear John Power, in a voice loud and clear, beg forgiveness of the people he had considered his tormentors for 42 years.*

There was the courage of Glen Randall, an attorney released by the impatient Powers, yet he appeared on his own to speak for them. There were the Kempton's, Glenn and Albert, of Tempe and Chandler, who went against the wishes of some of their own kin to appear on behalf of Tom and John Power. After the hearing, 83-year old Frank Wooten, of Willcox, a brother of a slain deputy and traditional leader of a bitterly anti-Power faction, courageously held out a hand of forgiveness to Tom and John Power. It took courage for board members, Mr. Hoffman, W.W. Skipper Dick and Attorney General Wade Church, to recommend clemency, and it took courage for Governor Paul Fannin to grant the release.

After the crowd was cleared, Reverend Hoffman handed Tom and John Power their release papers which indicated that their sentence had been commuted from the rest of their natural life to "time served." Then on April 27th of 1960 Tom and John Power were released. They were both given $15 each as a clothing allowance. They were also given

$7.50 in cash and they were issued a 300 mile but ticket, but they did not need the ticket because their longtime friends Lee Solomon and Ted Mullin came to pick them up so they stopped at the Greyhound Bus depot in Florence and redeemed their tickets for $40 in cash. They gave the $40 they got for the tickets to Lee and Ted for the price of gasoline, to cover the expenses of driving the Power brothers to Bob Wheelers ranch near Kirkland Junction where Lee Solomon was foreman and where the brothers had a place to live and a job working as cowboys on the ranch.

Below is great article written by Bob Thomas, a reporter for the Tucson Daily Star Newspaper on April 27th 1960 the day the Power brothers left the Arizona State Prison in Florence, Arizona.

Tom and John Power receive their freedom

After serving 42 years of a life sentence

Florence, April 27, 1960-John and Tom Power left the Arizona State Prison with their freedom Wednesday morning with their belongings and the congratulations of their friends. They left behind 42 gray years of their lives. "We've been waiting for this day, God have we been waiting," Tom said. "What's holding us up now? Let's go," John Power told Tom and the others that were gathered there at the gate of the prison. The two old timers, famous in Arizona as the Power Brothers, left prison officially after winning parole last week. They served 42 years of a life sentence for the first degree murder of three lawmen they shot, on a cold, early morning on Feb. 10th 1918.

The long-remembered gunfight at the Powers' cabin in Keilburg Canyon in the Galiuro Mountains set several marks. It brought back capital punishment which had been outlawed in the state two years before: it brought out a record posse of 3,000 men who scoured Arizona and Old Mexico for 29 days; and it brought a record of 42-years imprisonment for the brothers, which was the longest prison sentence served in Arizona History, not to mention that the 29 days they were in flight and the 3,000 men in the field on their hunt was the longest and largest manhunt also in Arizona history.

But memories were just memories yesterday, John 70, and Tom 68, were caught up in the somewhat frustrating red tape of drumming a man out of prison. Warden Frank Eyman made it as easy as possible for the two men to slip easily back into the cowboy life they once knew. They had their prison possessions packed, new cowboy hats, Levis, and blue denim shirts and new cowboy boots they purchased in Florence and had their "release" picture taken by the prison photographer. But each time they thought they were read to leave one would remember something he had forgot. Warden Eyman said, "Tom was so excited, I finally had to dress him. He put on his boots but forgot his socks."

They received $12.50 each in cash as "mustering out pay" and a 300-mile one-way bus ticket to a destination of their choice. Tom received $44 for the items he made in prison to be sold to visitors and

John received $354 for the items he made and sold to visitors. In addition, John had over $12,000 of savings of which $10,000 was willed to him by Tom Sisson, the Powers' hired hand, who stuck with the Power brothers even though the brothers claim he had no part in the shooting. To Sisson the life sentence was an actuality; he died behind bars in 1957 at the age of 86. Tom managed to save $1,000 while imprisoned. Money however was no concern yesterday.

"I felt ten years younger," Tom said and breathed in a deep breath of fresh air. "Let's get the hell out of here," John said nervously. They had jobs along with a place to hang their hats at the AC Ranch near Kirkland Junction. Lee Solomon, an old friend who never abandoned them through the years, is foreman of the spread and said the boys can have a place there as long as they wish. Lee and Ted Muller, an ex-warden at the State Prison, came from Kirkland Junction to drive Tom and John Power back to the AC Ranch. Lee Solomon was very displeased at the publicity given the case.

"Just leave the boys be. They're going to have a hard time living normal lives," he said to a reporter waiting outside the prison walls that morning to interview the brothers. He said Walter Hoffman, the chairman of the board of pardons and paroles, had given strict orders that the brothers refrain from taking an active part in any TV, magazine or newspaper interview. "They're on parole, remember," Solomon said. They can be taken back to *jail if they break any rules. A small gnarled old cowpuncher, Solomon made friends with the Power family when they first arrived at Klondyke before Arizona became a state. "They were the scabbiest looking outfit I ever did see. Old wobbly wagons and skinny stock and old plow horses," Solomon went on to say, "I was punching cattle near Klondyke and I knew both sides of the story. Kane Wooten told me personally that he was going to shoot the hell out of the Powers' and become the next sheriff of Graham County.*

Kane Wooten, a deputy sheriff; Martin Kempton, another deputy, and Graham County Sheriff Robert F. McBride as well as Jeff Power, the father of the brothers, were all killed in the furious shootout. Only one officer, U.S. Deputy Marshal Frank Haynes, escaped unscathed. The posse attempted to arrest the brothers for being draft evaders during World War I. The shooting occurred at dawn on Feb. 10th 1918 when the posse surrounded the Power cabin. The brothers said the posse opened fire first and shot down their father as he stood in front of the cabin door with his hands raised and his gun lying on the ground beside him. They said they had been feuding with Kane Wooten and that he led the posse to their cabin that morning. Of course Haynes and relatives of the slain officers said the Powers' opened fire first.

Pressure brought by these relatives is believed to have kept the boys in prison after their only other parole hearing eight years ago. In an emotional parole hearing a week ago Wednesday the same relatives failed to keep the Powers' in prison when Lorenzo Wright, an ex-warden at the prison and former state president of the Church of Latter-day Saints tongue-whipped the brothers and sisters into asking forgiveness. The public repentance apparently swung the scales of justice in the Powers' favor in the minds of the parole board. The day they recommended parole, Governor Paul Fannin, signed their sentences commuted to time served. Both brothers indicated they may split up eventually with John going to Silver City, New Mexico to look up their brother Charles and Tom indicated he might head on over to Snyder, Texas to look up old friends and see if they still live in the area. "Come on, your old sour apple, you," Solomon told Tom Power, "I've got this old mean bronco that I've been saving for you to break."

While they were working on the AC Ranch near Kirkland Junction one Saturday afternoon Lee Solomon took them to the Elks Lodge in nearby downtown Prescott, Arizona to socialize and have a few cocktails. While they were there the manager gave them each a membership application. Lee talked them into joining and said it was a great fraternal organization and that he had been a member for over 30 years. Tom and John decided to go ahead and join. They filled out the applications, paid the membership fee and gave the applications back to the manager. About a half hour later the secretary of the lodge came back to speak to the brothers, He said;

"I hate to tell you this, but I must. The lodge has turned down your application for membership because you both are not citizens of this country."

Obviously John and Tom were furious. Tom said to Lee and John;

"Is it ever going to end."

When Tom got back to the ranch, Tom inquired about how they could get back their citizenship. All he and his brother wanted was to be able to cast a vote in the upcoming election. Below is a newspaper article that ran in the Copper Era newspaper that was published out of Clifton, Arizona and was also syndicated to the Tucson Daily Star and the Arizona Republic newspapers;

Power Brothers Bid for Full Freedom

"TO WHOM IT MAY CONCERN- Thomas J. and John Power request a hearing before the Board of Pardons and Paroles to obtain a full pardon." This ad, as required by law, has been running for a month in the Copper Era, a newspaper located in Clifton, Arizona.

Three years have passed since the Power brothers were released from the Arizona State Prison in Florence. Before and during the time of their hearing the Powers were accused of being unfit to live in society.

They had killed three of a four-man sheriff's posse that had surrounded their mountain cabin on a snowy dawn on February 10th, 1918. If capital punishment had been legal in Arizona at that time, the Powers would have swung as mad dog draft dodgers. Instead, the unlettered brothers were sent up for life. Politically powerful friends and survivors of the posse men saw to it that the Powers stayed in prison for 42 years, with only one clemency hearing, that is a farce.

Forgotten through all these years were the circumstances of the crime and the character of the convicts; that the motives of some of the posse men were personal; that testimony of the surviving officer was contradictory; that most probably the Powers' father was gunned down first. And finally, in 41 years, 11 months and 7 days, the Power brothers had caused no more harm to anybody.

Three former wardens pleaded for their release. And in April of 1960, the brothers were put out of prison on parole. John, at 72 the older, was living with friends near Silver City, New Mexico. He is wracked by what he calls rheumatism, no doubt arthritis, but he has supported himself by digging ditches for ranchers and clearing brush. He has continued to forge and mount in silver old-style spurs and bridle bits. In his battered truck he has returned to Arizona several times to visit his brother, living in Kirkland to push for a full pardon. Tom Power, the younger brother, has lived for the most part at the AC Ranch and has worked for their friend Lee Solomon and when it got slow he worked around the area as a cowboy.

Just recently he was working at the Phoenix City Horse Riding Stables, located in South Mountain Park, caring for a string of horses and guiding them on trail horseback rides. He has acquired a *few head of quarter horses. He breaks them and trains them to be work cattle. He hopes to someday own a small breeding ranch.*

Neither one of the brothers has received as much as a parking ticket in these past three years of conditional freedom. Those who might be in favor of continued parole may argue that the Powers are old men and need to be looked after. The Power brothers have show that this is absolutely not the case. They have lived and worked in society and do not need help from anybody. In fact, they want to make their own decisions. They say the record shows they have been law abiding good citizens even though they spent 42 years in prison and have caused nobody any trouble since they have been on parole.

Attorney Richardson, who spoke against the brothers at the first hearing from Safford talked with Don Welker, a Safford banker who was a member of the Parole board. Mr. Richardson did not wish John and Tom success in their efforts to be granted a pardon with the restoration of their citizenship. He was quoted as saying to Mr. Welker;

"There has never been a sheriff that ever recommended clemency for a man who had killed another sheriff."

Welker said;

"I don't know if that is true, I've got two such recommendations right here in my file.

He was referring to the recommendations we had received   from the sheriffs of Graham and Greenlee

Counties that were submitted to the Pardon and Parole Board the day they were granted their release. Tom Power said that he was really upset at the news media because they continued to say they were not considered citizens. He did not understand that as long as they were on parole they were still convicted felons and citizen rights are stripped for anyone convicted of a felony. Not only had they been railroaded at the trial but it did not seem that this nightmare would ever go away. He decided then that he was going to pursue all avenues to have his and John get their citizenship reinstated so they could cast votes in elections and finally be able to hold their heads high again.

His first move was to contact Bob Pickrell the current State Attorney General. After several calls and leaving messages he finally called Tom back. Tom explained his business and Mr. Pickrell told him that he was familiar with their case. He said he would go ahead and talk with the two members of the Parole board, W.W. "Skipper" Dick and the Reverend Hoffman to see if he could get their citizenship reinstated. Mr. Pickrell directed Tom to Mr. W.W. Drew, the Director of Parole Services in the state. He told Tom that Mr. Drew would instruct him as to what forms they needed to obtain and get the ball rolling.

Tom Power finally spoke with Mr. Drew, after leaving several telephone messages. He told Tom that in order to obtain a pardon he needed to ascertain recommendations from the judge and the county attorney in the county where they were convicted. Tom said he reminded Mr. Drew that all the people connected with their trial were long dead. Mr. Drew said that letters from these people's successors would suffice. Tom said that he and John, immediately after they hung up the phone, headed to Clifton, the capital city of Greenlee County where the trial took place.

They were able to obtain recommendations from the current Superior Court Judge, Ruskin Lines; Irval L. Mortensen, The Greenlee County Attorney; and Henry Bowman, The Greenlee County Sheriff, along with Jacque Felshaw, *"Aunt Jacque,"* Justice of the Peace in Pima, Arizona, who was familiar with the Power brothers case. Tom and John took the forms right back to Mr. Drew.

From that day Tom and John spent most of their free time living in Thatcher, always keeping the parole board updated as to their addresses but after many inquiries they heard nothing and wondered if their plight had been forgotten. John had a lot of health problems due to his arthritis and several accidents, so Tom was looking after him. Then on January 17th 1969, Tom and John were having a cup of coffee and turned on their radio to listen to the news. Suddenly, they heard their names mentioned. There was a full review of their past "crimes," along with the information that the Arizona Board of Pardons and Paroles had voted unanimously the day before to recommend that Governor Jack Williams grant Tom and John Power a full pardon, also reinstating their citizenship.

Later that day John Power was reading the newspaper and found an article explaining the circumstances surrounding the full pardon. Of course the paper still referred to them as draft dodgers and murderers, which really upset the men.

There were so many bad reports about them that they knew they would never be able to straighten out the real story. People that supposedly knew them wrote stories that were simply not true. The Power brothers were happy though that they would finally be vindicated for the crimes that supposedly they committed, and that was good enough for them. Their full pardon was signed and sealed by Governor Jack Williams on January 25th, 1969, nearly 51 years after, that fateful Sunday at their cabin in Kielburg Canyon.

Another great article that appeared in the Graham Examiner on September 12th 1970.

Power Brothers Cast their first Vote

Safford- Tom and John Power waited 52 years to cast a vote for the first time in their lives. In fact, voting was so important to them that in spite of illness they made a round trip of 120 miles, part of which was in an antiquated Jeep, to get to the polls. Tom, 77, had told friends when he received a pardon from the Arizona governor last February, "I want to see the day that I can vote."

He did. And then the following Friday morning September 11th, 1970, Tom Power died of a heart attack on the day of the 79th birthday of his brother John Power.

The sad story began back in 1918. There was a shootout at the Powers place in Kielburg Canyon near the town of Klondyke, in the middle of Graham County, Arizona. When the shooting was all over, Old Man Jeff Power was dead along with the Graham County Sheriff McBride and two of his deputies.

One side of the local legend was it that the Power brothers were resisting the draft. The sheriff and his men supposedly went out to see them about it. Another side held that a property feud between the Power clan and one of the deputies figured highly in the incident. At any rate, the Power brothers stood trial, were convicted of first degree murder and were sent to prison on life sentences.

Zola Claridge, a prominent business and political leader here was a young woman of 21 when the trial took place. She and her father operated a ranch in the same vicinity of the Power place. She said yesterday, "I attended every day of that trial and when it ended, I came away with one question in my mind. That was, where was the other side of the story? I only heard one side given at the trial."

Mrs. Claridge worked for many years to achieve a pardon and parole for Thomas Jefferson Power and John Grant Power. After several rejections the parole was granted in 1960. Then finally last February the Power brothers were pardoned. The first thing they did was go straight to the Graham County Courthouse in Safford and registered to vote. After registering they moved from Safford where they had been living, out to the Joe Bull Ranch, southwest of Bonita, a few miles from their pre-prison day's home.

Tuesday morning, they telephoned their friends, Marc and Zola Claridge, Tom said, "We sure would like to cast a vote." He didn't think, however, that the old jeep they were driving could make the trip all the way to Thatcher. They asked the Claridge's to them at the Bonita store. The Claridge's did. The Graham County Minority Republicans gained two votes, and the two old men gained the right to face the world as full fledged citizens of the United States.

Today at 4 pm on a hill near the ranch home they knew as young men, Tom

Power was buried. The simple service was held at the Klondyke cemetery. He lies in a plot beside his sister, Ola May Power and his grandmother, Martha Jane Power, who both died a little before the shootout.

The following article appeared in The Arizona Daily Star on November 23rd, 1975 written by reporter Pete Cowgill.

Klondyke-Getting old is hell, especially, for men who have lived and breathed in the outdoors all their lives. There are no "Green Valley Grins" on the faces of John Power, Lupe Salazar and Merle Haby-the three patriarchs of the town of Klondyke.

Power is 84. He lives in a trailer parked behind the general store-post office-post office in Klondyke. He drives an old pickup and cashes welfare checks. He was working a mining claim deep in the Galiuro Mountains more than twenty miles away. He has arthritis so bad now that he can't get to his claim anymore.

Salazar is 81. His teeth are excellent but his eyes are dim. He quit riding a horse and helping to work his ranch three years ago because of a bad knee and a rupture. His sons Bill and Tex and their families now are "punching cattle."

Haby is 77. He still climbs to the top of his windmills to fix them. His large, powerful hands which have made everything from violins to rifles are almost stilled. He can't see too clearly what he is doing.

An era is coming to an end. This is the era of the true outdoorsman, as different from his modern counterpart as the sunrise is from an electric light bulb.

Two years ago John Power went back to the mine and dug up the bones of his father which had been place in a cistern hole after the body had lain seven days in the mine tunnel. He took the bones of his father to the Klondyke Cemetery and buried them beside the rest of his family. He made headstones for the members of his family.

"I can't ride a horse anymore because of the arthritis in my knee and shoulder," John said, "But I've go to keep going." His new goal is to fix up the road they built and make it so he can drive his pickup to the mine. He says the mine cabin is still as good as new and the spring still produces cold, clean and clear water. He said he wants to live out his life on their homestead.

"I need an old Jeep," he says to this reporter. "Do you know where I can get a good one for $500?" Power's thinning hair is nearly white. His hands, like all men who have worked hard for many years, are wide and tough. His voice is soft and firm and on occasion he will smile. I asked him as we finished the interview,

Why don't you find a rich widow and get married, John? He answered loud and clear, "I've had enough troubles in my life, I'm not about to get tangled up with a woman. I simply don't have the patience to take on a woman."

The last newspaper article regarding the Power Brothers appeared in the Tucson Daily Star on April 6th, 1976

Shoot-Out Figure of WW1 Dies

When John Power did not pick up his mail yesterday at the post office in Klondyke, people began to wonder if he was alright. One of his friends, Bill Heard, a retired painter, stopped by the 85-year old man's trailer that was parked behind the Klondyke store and post office about 4 pm yesterday, and found him dead in his bed. It was thought that he died sometime during the night while in his sleep. "John Power had the flu," said Ray Luster, the owner of the Caldwell Funeral Home in Safford, where the funeral services are pending. "He'd been feeling quite poorly over the past week."

The final piece of the story of the most notorious gunfight on February 10th 1918 which took the lives of four men and brought about the largest manhunt in Arizona history, lasting 29 days with over 3,000 men, including army troops and finally the two brothers served the longest prison sentence in Arizona history, ended with the death of the last living participant, John Power.

It has been this author's pleasure to write the story of Tom and John Power. Two men this author met in July of 1966 in People's Valley, Arizona, on the back way to Prescott.

It's amazing that other authors of books about this story base their findings on talking with old timers in and around Safford, Arizona and yet this authors interview with Tom and John Power, also two old timers but two of men who actually lived this story, are even today, not accepted as fact along with relatives to this day, almost a hundred years later, in Safford still carry hatred, even though they never met these two harmless old men.

It is this authors hope that someday the people in Safford and the surrounding area, finally accept the fact that these two men were railroaded and served their time. Tom Power's apology to the victims of this shootout's family, at the time he and his brother were finally acquitted, should be good enough to put this story to bed and forgive the two brothers. None of the original individuals involved in this travesty are alive and if the state saw fit to release these men, that should be good enough.

Below is a forest service map of the Galiuro Wilderness Area including the Power Garden Cabin & the shootout Cabin

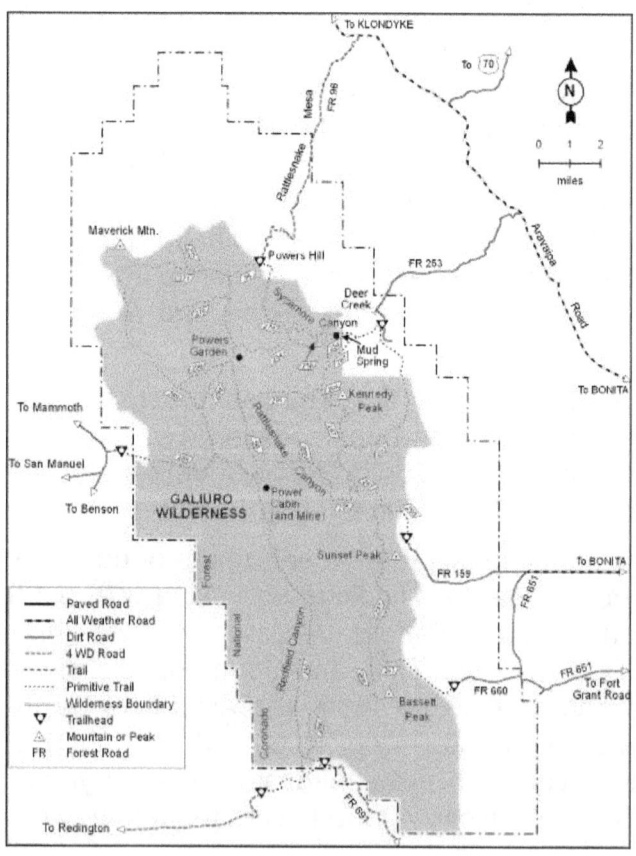

Bibliography

Shoot-Out at Dawn- An Arizona Tragedy- Written by Tom Power with John Whitlach

Authors interview with John and Tom Power. This author would like to thank Tom and John Power along with Lee Solomon for their personal conversation with this author and for to Tom Power for his amazing diary of his life. His recollection of the circumstances surrounding the gunfight and since he was an actual member of the shootout

The Evaders or Wilderness Shoot-Out- Written by Darvil B. McBride, son the slain Sheriff of Graham County- even though he was not an actual Witness thanks to Mr. McBride for his hard work in recreating the circumstances around the death of his father

Mike Conway and Nyle Niemuth, and The Arizona Mining and Gem Museum- for guiding me to the two publications that show how much ore (Gold and Silver) were recorded as being taken from the Rattlesnake mining District, from 1900 to 1980. The Gold Leaf Mine was the only mine that produced ore, it was always known as the Power Mine.

Wendy Goen, ERM- History and Archives Division Arizona State Library, Archives and Public Records for her work and diligence in finding supporting documents and photos for all my books.

Sharlot Hall Museum Archives- For finding old newspaper and magazine articles to support this story.

The Arizona Republic Newspaper-
  Special thanks to reporter Don Dedera for never
  giving up on the Power brothers and being the key
  person that helped them get out of prison and for
  them getting their pardon. Several articles.

The Tucson Daily Star Newspaper-
  Special thanks to their reporter Bob Thomas- who
  also never gave up on the Power brothers.
  Several articles.

The Graham Examiner Newspaper-
  Thanks to the reports printed by this newspaper
  even though the articles were quite biased.

The Graham County Recorder- Wendy John- for all
  her efforts in finding so many legal documents
  found in the county archives.

The Silver Belt Newspaper, published out of Globe
  Arizona. Various articles

About the Author;

William "Tom" Vyles aka Zeke Crandall was born in London, Ontario, Canada. The family moved to Phoenix, Arizona in 1956. A life long battle with Asthma, several bouts with pneumonia, in an out of hospitals the first nine years of life, the family was instructed by physicians to move to Arizona for the hot dry climate.

In and out of school until age ten, home schooled by his mother Elizabeth, reading "The Books of Knowledge," encyclopedia, Tom fell in love with history. With no family in Arizona, our family adopted elderly neighbors, Kenny and Mary Harris, as our Arizona grandparents.

Kenny worked in the stockyards in Cincinnati as a brand inspector for cattle coming from Arizona. He became friends of John Wayne, who brought his cattle through the stockyards in Cincinnati. John talked Kenny into moving to Arizona. Kenny was a professional fiddle player, along with his friend Rudy Mack, who played banjo, they toured Arizona playing gigs.

Young Tom went along on most of the out of town music gigs. His job was to set up instruments and equipment. The carrot for Tom was that Kenny would take me rabbit and quail hunting the next day. Young Tom fell in love with Arizona history, because Kenny introduced him to many amazing older men, who told him stories of the old west.

Five other current books are available by this author through our website, www.arizonatales.com or email, zekecrandall46@hotmail.com